"Not the Christmas present you expected, Anne?"

"Or wanted, as I'm sure you're aware," she retorted, conscious of the interest their conversation was creating.

How could he do this to her? Anger began to replace her initial confusion over seeing Steele again, and she had to struggle to maintain control.

"All right, let's get this over with," she said. "You're here...I can see that. And I presume there's some reason for it, although I can't for the life of me imagine what it might be."

He remained unmoved by her attitude, seemed, if anything, to be enjoying it. "I came to take you to lunch."

"Ten thousand miles, just to take me to lunch?" she said sweetly. "That's a bit extravagant even for you, wouldn't you say?"

Victoria Gordon is a former radio, television and print journalist who began writing romances in 1979. Canadian-born, she moved to Australia in the early 1970s and now lives in northern Tasmania. The founding president of the Tasmanian Gundog Trial Association, she judges retrieving trials for gundogs and is active in a variety of other outdoor activities when not busy at her magical word processor.

Books by Victoria Gordon

Don't miss any of our special offers. Write to us at the following address for information on our newest releases.

Harlequin Reader Service
U.S.: 3010 Walden Ave., P.O. Box 1325, Buffalo, NY 14269
Canadian: P.O. Box 609, Fort Erie, Ont. L2A 5X3

GIFT-WRAPPED
Victoria Gordon

Harlequin Books

TORONTO • NEW YORK • LONDON
AMSTERDAM • PARIS • SYDNEY • HAMBURG
STOCKHOLM • ATHENS • TOKYO • MILAN
MADRID • WARSAW • BUDAPEST • AUCKLAND

This one's for Chris and Kaarin,
who shouldn't take it literally

ISBN 0-373-03342-7

GIFT-WRAPPED

Copyright © 1993 by Victoria Gordon.

CHAPTER ONE

SNOW had frosted his inky hair, giving Anne a preview of how Steele Murdoch might look when he got older.

That was her first impression, and it was so completely irrelevant to the situation that she almost laughed out loud. But then he spoke, and there was so much she remembered in that deep, velvet voice that she shivered despite the warmth around her.

'Hello, Wombat; you're looking fit and well,' he said, one dark eyebrow cocked as those sooty eyes roved up and down her body with a proprietorial smugness.

Wombat! Would she never be allowed to forget? That thought raced through her mind, but her body was reacting to his gaze, not to his words.

His glance was at once a caress and an accusation. He was seeing her, Anne thought, not as she stood but as she had once lain, pleading with him to take her, to join their bodies, their minds, their lives, to make her truly his.

Again she shivered, and this time he admitted noticing.

'You could invite me inside,' he said softly. 'I can't imagine this draught will be much good for your crop of rug-rats.'

Anne met his eyes, then dropped her own almost in a gesture of submission. Invite him in? It was the last, absolutely the *last* thing she wanted. But had she any choice? Not really, she decided quickly.

'All right, but I would remind you that I'm working,' she replied, determined to assert her authority while knowing she might just as well try to fly. Steele Murdoch acknowledged no authority but his own, as she knew only too well.

'They don't give you time for lunch?' he asked in a show of innocence she was far too experienced to accept. Anne thought quickly, desperately.

'I've been,' she told him then, hoping against hope that he wouldn't notice the lie, or at least wouldn't force the issue. Anne knew herself to be among the world's worst liars.

'OK,' he answered, then paused, allowing the silence to work on his behalf, letting her stew, letting her wonder what on earth he was doing here. And why.

Anne took it just as long as she could, and, while that seemed like hours, she knew her own hesitation to be only momentary. It wasn't so much that she *wanted* to break the silence; it was that anything was better than just having Steele undress her with his eyes.

He didn't just look through her clothing to see the slender figure beneath; his black, black eyes seemed able to look deeper than that, able to penetrate her every veil of privacy, to see right into her soul.

She turned silently away and stalked towards the very questionable privacy of her office, aware that he was watching her, equally aware that Karen, Linda and Helen, her assistants at the day-care centre, were watching *him*.

She preceded him into the tiny cubicle, suddenly aware of just how small, how shabby it really was. Steele closed the door behind them without being asked, then took it upon himself also to shed the bulky sheepskin coat he wore.

'You won't be staying long enough for that,' said Anne, then halted as she realised how totally rude her statement had been. 'I'm sorry,' she added lamely, but then found she had no other words to add.

'This thing's too hot *outside*, let alone in here,' he said with a grimace. 'I can't understand how you lot manage with this central heating...it just can't be healthy.'

Under the heavy coat he wore only a light woollen turtle-neck, and its ivory colour served to set off the darkness of his tan. Below the sweater he wore sharply creased trousers, and Anne knew without looking that his feet would be encased in custom-made boots.

She had already settled herself gingerly behind her small desk, grateful for the modicum of security it afforded her. Steele slung his coat over the back of the office's only other chair, then seated himself and looked towards her expectantly.

Between them, silence hung like a tangible curtain until he finally grinned with apparent satisfaction and then spoke.

'You seem...somewhat taken aback,' he offered. 'Is it because I didn't bounce in with a sack over my shoulder crying Merry Christmas or *Joyeux Noël*, or whatever?'

Anne fought for control, fought to keep the sarcasm out of her reply. He'd be expecting it, she knew that. Steele Murdoch loved nothing better than to get her going; he said anybody could get her goat—it must be the slowest one around.

'You must admit to being something of a surprise,' she finally replied.

'Hah! Not the Christmas present you most expected, eh?' he chuckled.

'Or wanted, as I'm sure you're aware,' she retorted quickly, all too aware now of the interest their conversation was creating from outside the office.

How could he *do* this to her? The other three girls would get through the rest of the winter on this, Anne thought. She could just imagine the prying and probing and damnable speculation she was in for. Anger began to replace her initial confusion, and she had to struggle to maintain control.

'All right, let's get this over with,' she said with a shake of her head. 'You're here...I can see that. And I presume there's some reason for it, although I can't for the life of me imagine what it might be.'

He remained unmoved by her attitude, seemed to be enjoying it, if anything.

'I came to take you to lunch,' he growled. 'I told you that.'

Anne had to grin at the mock-fierceness, at his habitual refusal to take anything seriously if he didn't choose to.

'Ten thousand miles, just to take me to lunch?' she queried. 'That's a bit extravagant even for you, wouldn't you say?'

'Well, there *is* a bit more to it than that,' he admitted without a hint of contrition, but then halted without adding any explanation.

Anne waited. He was playing, she knew, toying with her, baiting her deliberately. And it was a game she'd decided she would not play.

'Heard from the old fellow recently?'

Steele asked the question with deceptive innocence. Anne cringed inside, knowing that he knew she hadn't written to her father in nearly a year, knowing he knew she ought to feel guilty, knowing he'd make sure she *would* feel guilty even if she didn't just now.

'Not . . . recently,' she hedged. 'But then the mails are never much chop at this time of year.' Not a lie, exactly, but close enough to make her uncomfortable about it. She wouldn't, Anne told herself, put herself in such a position with anybody else.

Steele's reply was a grunt. He didn't even bother to take her up on the deliberate attempt to mislead. Twisting in his chair, he reached into an inner pocket of the jacket behind him, extracted a small packet, and pitched it expertly on to the desk before her.

'Still haven't grown up, I see,' he muttered, and before Anne could reply he had lifted the coat, shrugged into it, and was turning towards the office door. 'So I won't waste any more of your time. Merry Christmas.'

'No . . . wait!' Anne was on her feet now, rushing round the desk and reaching out to grasp at his sleeve. She couldn't let him leave like this, with no explanation, even, of why he'd come all the way from Tasmania in Australia to Edmonton, in Canada, and at *this* time of year!

Steele eyed her hand on his sleeve, looking at her slender fingers, she thought, with the same expression he'd use for one of the gigantic huntsman spiders so common in the Australian bush.

She had never wanted to see him again, and told herself that really she still didn't. But now that he was here she just *had* to know why, had to force from him the latest news of her father. If he hadn't come, she realised suddenly, she could have gone on without continued contact—but now that he was here it all seemed to have a vastly different emphasis.

'Please,' she said, adding her broadest smile to the plea, 'you can't go without...well...without at least telling me how things are, how...how my father is, and——'

'This is neither the time nor the place,' he said. 'And, since you've already had lunch, I guess it will just have to wait.'

'Wait? Wait until when?'

'Until I'm ready to tell you, I guess,' Steele replied with a grin that matched his name. It was cold, formal, with not even a hint of the friendliness that had been there when he first arrived.

'I...but...how will I know?' Anne stammered. 'I mean...well...where are you staying? You could at least tell me that.'

'I could.' He nodded, the gesture suggestive of a wise owl, but hardly that benign. He could tell her, but obviously he wasn't going to.

Anne didn't know what to say, what to do. She couldn't just let him walk out like this. What if he didn't come back? And it would be just like Steele Murdoch, she thought, to do exactly that, to get her attention and then leave her hanging.

'Or wouldn't it be frustrating if I just went walk-about?' he asked with a wolf's grin, reading her mind with that uncanny skill he had. 'I might, too. After all, I've done what I came to do, which was to deliver your Christmas present from the old fellow.'

'God, you're spiteful,' she asserted hotly, angered at having been taken in yet again by this cunning, devious man. 'I know you hate me, but that's no reason to indulge in this...this...torture.'

'Hate you? What a strange idea.' Steele laughed, but there was little humour in his eyes as he gazed down at her. Anne felt suddenly as if she wasn't even significant enough for such a strong emotion as hate. 'And I'd hardly call it torture to bring you a Christmas present from halfway round the world—unless of course you just can't bear to abide by the sticker that says not to open it until Christmas.'

'That's not what I meant and you know it,' Anne snapped. She hadn't even looked at the parcel, which lay where he'd pitched it. And she wouldn't, not while he was there to watch her, to read her mind as easily as if she'd been writing her thoughts on a blackboard for anybody to read.

'How can you expect me to know what you mean?' he asked, his voice soft with professed innocence. 'It's been ... what ... nearly two years? That's a long time to keep track of how anybody thinks, especially ... well ...'

He shrugged his shoulders, broader than usual with the bulk of the sheepskin jacket, but, instead of following through to elaborate on his teasing pause, once again he turned towards the door.

'How about a drink after work, then?' Anne heard herself asking. It wasn't at all what she'd intended to say, and she found herself adding lamely, 'I can find time, I guess,' just to keep it from sounding too wishy-washy, too obliging.

'Oh, I wouldn't want you to put yourself out,' was the calm, icy reply. Steele's eyes were as cold as his voice, and she felt herself almost cringing beneath their intensity.

But, she decided, she'd made her gesture of conciliation and he'd have to take it or leave it. Anything further and he'd have her begging. She felt guilty, if justified, in letting communications lapse between her and her father—not that it was any of Steele Murdoch's business anyway!—but not so guilty that she would let this autocratic man dictate to her conscience.

'If it were a matter of that, I wouldn't have suggested it,' she replied staunchly. And found herself wishing he'd just accept or refuse—and quickly— before she lost all control of both temper and composure.

'You're sure you've got time?'

'I just said so,' she said firmly, trying not to show the suspicion she felt. He was leading up to something; this man, she knew, could teach courses in being devious, and was at his worst when he sounded most plausible.

'No boyfriend waiting to collect you after work? I'm a bit surprised at that,' he continued, obviously leading her, trying for a reaction.

Anne wasn't going to bite. She told herself that, mentally, before making any reply. 'I'll have to spend most of this afternoon putting them all off,' she said finally, 'but since you've come all this way it's only fair, I suppose...'

'Spare me,' he growled. Anne felt that tiny thrill of victory, of having finally got at least some of her own back—until he continued!

'Logically, then, you can just as easily make yourself free for dinner, rather than just a drink,' he said, not making it a question, much less an invitation. No, not Steele Murdoch. He spoke as if it was a simple statement of fact, unarguable.

'I...well...I...' Anne stammered, her mind racing, seething with a mixture of indignation and frustration at having been so easily trapped. Damn him!

'Shall I collect you here, then, or would you rather go home and change first?' he continued, nothing in his expression revealing any awareness of her confusion.

Anne struggled for an excuse—any excuse! But it was futile and she knew it. If she begged off now, he'd be just mean enough to take her at her word and disappear as mysteriously as he'd come, leaving her wondering forever why he'd come at all.

'Or is it one of those nights you just *have* to wash your hair?' he asked with a wry grin, and reached out to touch her hair before she could retreat.

His fingers were as gentle as she remembered—mustn't remember!—and the gesture was too familiar even after all this time. She felt herself wanting to lean into his touch, to revel in it.

'It doesn't feel dirty to me,' he said, and now his words were barely audible, his voice was so quiet. Anne shivered inwardly at the allure of that voice, and cursed herself for it.

'I wasn't trying to make excuses,' she snapped, yanking herself back to reality and in the process pulling away from his touch. 'It's just that—well, it *is* rather unexpected, after all. I didn't come to work this morning with any plans for going out, and you haven't given me any indication of where you'd want to go, so I can hardly be blamed for wondering if I'm properly dressed, or—or—well, whatever!'

She felt the first pang of a different guilt then. She *had* planned to go out after work, but of course that was with John. Dear, dear John, who didn't care what

she wore, who wouldn't, in any event, take her anywhere that what she wore would make the slightest
difference——

Who wouldn't take her anywhere at all, if it weren't
for her ability to pay the tab, she thought suddenly,
and winced at the betrayal involved in such thinking.
It wasn't John's fault, after all. He couldn't help being
out of work. Times were tough, especially for
somebody who had always had the system against
him.

She'd have to telephone him, she realised. And
fairly quickly, too, or he'd be off somewhere with his
friends and she'd never find him until it was too late.

'I might leave the choice to you,' Steele was saying.
'I've only been exposed to what's handy to where I'm
staying, and you should have a better idea of what's
good; it's your town, after all.'

Her town? In the context of his comment, it was
anything but, Anne thought, remembering his taste
for quality. She and Steele had dined out fairly often
during her Tasmanian experience, but she realised now
that she'd not done anything even remotely similar
since her return to Edmonton. Partly because of the
cost, of course, but also because John always felt uncomfortable in really good restaurants, or so he said.
He didn't like snooty waiters, didn't like having to
dress up—didn't, to her knowledge, even have the
clothes to dress up in—and their evenings out usually
involved groups of his choosing in places where she
wouldn't be caught dead with somebody like Steele
Murdoch.

Once again Anne felt a twinge of disloyalty, but she
hadn't time now to indulge in that. Her mind was

awhirl with the task of resolving this situation quickly, and without losing face.

'There are several excellent places in the West Edmonton Mall,' she said quickly, grasping at the first answer that came to mind. 'That's something you ought to see anyway, while you're here. It's billed as the eighth wonder of the modern world—the biggest shopping centre under one roof anywhere.' Once started, she used that as a springboard to solving the other part of the problem facing her.

'How about I meet you there at, say, eight o'clock?' she asked. 'Much easier that way, since where I live would make it ridiculously inconvenient for you to collect me . . .' She trailed off, realising with acute embarrassment that she was blathering, making very little sense, considering she didn't know where he was staying or what transportation he might have. But the gigantic Mall was a perfect choice, she thought suddenly. At the very least, there would be people around, probably thousands upon thousands of them, this close to Christmas. They wouldn't need a booking at that hour—it was late for Edmontonians *she* knew to be dining, and there was all the choice in the world.

'OK, eight o'clock, then,' he replied—too quickly? Anne had a flash of suspicion, but it was submerged by the sheer relief that she now didn't have to worry about him showing up at her dingy, grotty little bed-sitter flat. She'd never paid much attention, until just this minute, to how truly awful the tiny flat really was, and for an instant she felt, not guilt, but a whimsy of being able to use where she lived to demonstrate the success of her lifestyle, somewhere that made a statement about *her*!

There was a rueful thought that the flat did just that—but it wasn't a statement she liked very much. It was cheap, but nobody could say much of anything else favourable about the place.

Anne shook her head, trying to bring every thought into some semblance of logic. 'Eight o'clock, yes,' she finally said. 'I'll meet you—uhm——' her mind raced frantically as she searched for some logical meeting spot in the vastness of the hundred-acre-plus complex '—how about at the entrance to the water park? You shouldn't have any problem finding that . . . any cabbie in the city will know where to take you, and——'

'I'll manage,' he interjected. 'And as to the question of dress . . .' he paused, his eyes roving down her slim figure from the crown of auburn hair to the pale mauve blouse, the black skirt that suddenly seemed to fit too snugly, and on down the length of her legs '. . . let's keep it to just *medium* posh, eh? I'll find a tie somewhere—I might even have brought one with me—and you can govern yourself accordingly; I'm sure you'll manage to look fine.'

He was through the door before she could think of a suitable reply, leaving her standing with her mouth half open and her mind adrift in a sea of apprehension and confusion. The butterflies in her stomach all took wing once he'd gone, and she had to hang on to the edge of her desk as she worked her way round to where she could sit down.

'Amazing,' she muttered aloud, staring down at her trembling fingers and forcing herself to draw slow, deep breaths as she struggled for control.

Through the side-window of her office she could see her three assistants huddled in conversation, quite ignoring the children they were paid to watch. Anne got to her feet, determined to put a stop to this nonsense immediately, but even as she did so the girls separated and resumed their duties.

Anne sat down again, and stayed for a moment with eyes closed as she fought to balance her feelings. How typical of Steele Murdoch, she thought, to drop back into her life like a thunderbolt. Not for him the niceties of a warning letter, or a telephone call, much less the decency to wonder if she'd want to see him or not!

And she hadn't wanted to see him. Definitely had not! Which was easy to say, but nowhere as easy as it would have been yesterday, before his physical presence made such a pronouncement questionable, to say the least.

I don't want to see him, she told herself, so why the hell did I agree to meet him . . . and for dinner, no less?

Just the thought of it gave her a headache, and she wished beyond hoping that she could manage to get through the afternoon without the typical and usual crises that went with her job.

First things first; she must get on the phone immediately and break her date with John. She would have to make some excuse and hope he'd accept it without too much question. A straight-out lie went against the grain, but what choice did she have? She hardly fancied the task of explaining why she absolutely *had* to go for dinner with a man John had never even heard of!

It wasn't John's jealousy she feared, although that was an aspect which bore considering. John was seldom jealous, as such. It was just that his level of self-esteem was very fragile, and Anne couldn't bear the thought of deliberately hurting him.

The problem was going to be finding some plausible excuse for putting off their dinner tonight, and it was complicated by the shortage of alternatives, with Christmas so close. She stewed about it for a few minutes, then decided to stay with the truth. The situation was bad enough, she thought, without adding lying as a further complication.

'A friend of my father,' she found herself saying a few moments later, having luckily managed to catch John on the verge of departing for an afternoon with friends at the pool hall.

'It isn't anything I have much choice over,' she explained patiently after listening to a litany of objections. 'He's sent along a Christmas present, and I can't very well refuse dinner and just ask that it be delivered, can I?'

Tell the truth and shame the devil, she thought after John was finally pacified. But what result from bending the truth into a pretzel? Her journey into self-examination was cut short by afternoon coffee and the no-win situation of having to provide some explanation about her visitor.

'Australia, eh? Wish *my* father had friends like that, no matter where,' was Karen's comment, delivered with a perceptive smirk. 'And he's come all this way just to see you? No wonder you were a bit edgy this morning.' The other girls, at least for the moment, were less bitchy about it. Steele Murdoch was described by Helen and Linda—for once in total agreement—as gorgeous, devilishly handsome and utterly splendid.

Karen, as usual more candid than decorous, ended by saying, 'He can park his pyjamas under my pillow any time. If *he's* any example of what's available in Australia, I'm surprised you ever came back. I wouldn't have!'

You would if you'd been in my shoes, Anne thought. And would have found herself wishing she could put the cheeky Karen into her shoes tonight, if such a thought wasn't so patently ridiculous.

She had a moment's fantasy of Steele Murdoch, faced with Karen saying, 'Anne sent me to take her place,' and almost laughed out loud.

But the humour was short-lived, especially when Karen noticed it and maliciously misinterpreted it. 'I bet *he's* the reason for this Christmas moodiness,' Anne overheard her remark to the other girls. 'Bet he was supposed to come *last* Christmas, or else he didn't send her a present.'

'There's one this year, though. I saw it on her desk,' added Linda, and whatever Helen was going to contribute was stillborn when they realised Anne could hear them.

If only you knew, Anne thought. You'd sing a different tune then, and it wouldn't be utterly splendid either. After which she uttered a silent prayer of thanks that they *didn't* know, and she hoped they never would.

The rest of the day dragged. The children were unusually obstreperous, probably, Anne thought, because the other three girls were as distracted by Steele Murdoch's visit as she herself had been. Or else the children were just picking up her own pendulum-like emotions and reacting accordingly. She often had the feeling that children were born psychic, and, much as she loved them, there were times—like this—when it was a royal pain.

Anne had thought she might use her position of authority to steal an hour off—she was certainly owed plenty—so as to get home with loads of time to prepare herself for the evening. In the end, however, she didn't dare; there was already far too much speculation about her surprise visitor, and the very last thing she wanted was to add to it by giving her three assistants more to gossip about.

She was already running late, therefore, by the time the final child had been collected by parents also running late because of the Christmas crowds and the snowy weather. Anne too was hampered by the weather. Brisk winds from the morning had slackened, but the snow itself had become thicker; turgid, heavy snowflakes blanketed everything, and it took ten minutes just to clear sufficient snow from her ageing Volkswagen so that she could see to drive home in the poor conditions.

Steele Murdoch must be loving this, she thought. What a terrible change from the long, hot summer days he would have traded for this blizzard. The car radio told her it was warmer than when she'd driven to work that morning, but the difference was so minimal as to be irrelevant. She remembered her early days in Tasmania—in the midst of their so-called winter, where it hardly ever got below freezing and yet the forecasters went on and on about wind-chill factors that were at best picayune by Canadian standards.

Still, she thought as the car fought a losing battle between keeping the windscreen clear and her feet unfrozen at the same time, there was something to be said for a winter where snow was rare enough to be a delightful novelty instead of a daily drudgery.

And, while Steele Murdoch might whinge about central heating, Anne could only bless it as she entered her tiny flat to the welcoming warmth. Brushing the snow off her boots and jacket before they became totally sodden, she gazed round the dingy room with a feeling of depression. The place was clean enough—she spent enough time scrubbing and polishing on weekends that it ought to be—but no amount of cleaning could make up for the sheer decrepitude of the tiny flat. There wasn't room enough for her books, which were stacked almost everywhere. There was too much room for her clothes, because she didn't have that many. And on the bad days there was too much room for Anne herself, because somehow then there was plenty of space for the loneliness and bleakness and boredom of her life to crouch in there with her.

'Yuck!' She twisted her lips around the word as she stood in the entryway and glared around her with derision. It wasn't the first time she'd looked at the flat like that, but it was the first time she'd admitted just how *nowhere* her life was, how purposeless and mundane it all was.

She had a brief mental picture of having to bring Steele Murdoch here, and shrugged the thought away as too horrid to contemplate. Even his rough-and-ready hunting shack on the mountain adjoining her father's farm was better than this, she thought. More primitive, certainly, but infinitely better.

The shack had no indoor plumbing, no proper electricity, and quite rudimentary, wood-fired cooking and heating, but it also had personality, warmth, and a feeling of belonging. It squatted in a small clearing, overlooking the Broadmarsh valley below and to the north, and even in winter it greeted the occasional high-country snow with an aura of stolid permanence.

Like its owner, she thought. Steele didn't merely accept; what he didn't like, he changed. He had made his own world, largely in his own mould, and his weekend retreat was only one element, one aspect, of the man himself.

Only one element . . . one of many, many indeed in a man so complex that it was questionable if even *he* really understood the entire Steele Murdoch.

Certainly, Anne thought as she rushed through her shower, careful to keep from getting her hair wet, *she* didn't even begin to understand him. Right from their very first meeting, Steele Murdoch had managed to keep her well and truly off-balance.

And he'd be trying his best to do it again tonight, she realised, despite being on *her* home ground, in *her* city and *her* country!

'Well, good luck, mate!' she sneered into the mirror as she carefully applied the bare minimum of make-up, then suddenly realised she was doing *that* to his taste, and plastered more on just to be difficult.

She was less adventurous with regard to what she wore, but mostly because there wasn't enough choice to make the exercise interesting. Anne's only suitable outfits were her 'basic black' cocktail dress and a slightly more *risqué* dress in a shade of green which perfectly suited her redhead's complexion. She didn't own a proper evening gown, since the only one she'd ever owned or needed—and which Steele had seen anyway, in Australia—no longer fitted a figure which had grown slimmer on her return to Canada.

No, she decided, the overdone make-up would have to be enough rebellion. She wasn't going to make a complete fool of herself in public even to spite him! So it was the basic black, with lightly patterned tights and patent court shoes to match. She had to tuck the shoes into her coat pockets; she would drive in her snowboots and change when she was parked at the Mall.

There was just sufficient room in her evening bag for the still-wrapped parcel she had remembered to collect from her desk before leaving work that evening. She would ensure, at least, that Steele knew she had enough intestinal fortitude to leave the present wrapped as instructed, even if she had to wave the thing in his face to prove it.

'And if it were heavier I'd hit you over the head with it,' she vowed with a final, determined glare in the mirror before returning to the cold, blowing snow and her fractious vehicle.

Even with the best of intentions, she was five minutes late arriving at the Mall, and she lost an additional five minutes searching for a parking slot which would allow her to get into the complex without walking a ridiculous distance in her flimsy shoes.

Inside, she found herself part of a swirling, bustling throng of Christmas shoppers, all seemingly going in several directions at once; just negotiating her way through the crowds to where Steele Murdoch was to meet her became a mammoth exercise.

She couldn't remember ever being in such a crowd, and she wondered as she struggled through the swarms of people how Steele Murdoch must be reacting. He was not at all a crowd person, and indeed Anne had heard him comment that he wouldn't stand in a crowd of ten thousand people to witness the Second Coming.

'Which is about all that's missing here,' she muttered to herself after having her toes stepped on for the third time.

Eventually, however, she reached the designated meeting place, and was pleased to see that Steele had got there first and was waiting with apparent patience. He'd changed to a dark suit and gleaming white shirt which set off his tan to perfection. And, as Anne might have expected, he wasn't obviously impatient, but stood calmly watching the antics of the people in the water park with its multitude of slides.

He'd have been there on time, she knew. Probably a few minutes early, even, since he prized punctuality. She did too, but seemed doomed to perpetual failure when it came to achieving it. There was always something . . .

Now, despite being late, she used her unseen vantage-point to just stand and observe the man who'd allegedly come ten thousand miles just to take her to lunch. It wouldn't, she knew, be anywhere near that simple. With Steele Murdoch, nothing ever was. He'd have come to Edmonton for some other reason, and her own part in the overall plan might be obvious or obscure, but it would have been *planned*.

Watching him from the relative concealment of a pillar, with crowds swirling between them, she couldn't help but notice how he seemed to create a space around himself—his own space of privacy, of self. It wasn't that he was overtly aggressive or anything. It was simply that he seemed to exist in a larger-than-life aura.

As she watched, two stunningly beautiful young women, both attired in the latest of fashion, slowed to make their own not-so-discreet appraisal of Steele, who responded in kind with a raised eyebrow and a subtle but distinct nod of approval. Anne's own re-action was a definite snort of annoyance, followed as quickly by a flicker of further annoyance—this time at herself—for allowing herself to be bothered by such antics. He was, she had to admit, a mightily good-looking man, but that had nothing to do with her; she didn't care any more, and wasn't, she told herself, at all interested.

She hovered then, torn between the desire to walk over and join him, to have their meal together, to get it all over and done with—and the very real pleasure she found in being able to watch him, unobserved, from a position of comparative safety.

He was watching the activities around him, but to Anne's mind he wasn't really paying great attention. He seemed vaguely distracted, out of focus with his surroundings. She would have liked to think it was because of impatience for her arrival, but she didn't dare believe that. And when she finally did abandon her observer's role, finally walked over to confront this best-forgotten, unforgettable enigma from the past, it was to find he had indeed been distracted. Even as she approached, it was to find his dark eyes blank, his mind obviously far from the vibrant, pre-Christmas throngs that surrounded him, the hundreds of people sporting in the midwinter wonder of the water world.

'I'm late,' she said in greeting. Better to make the admission before he had the chance.

It was a gesture wasted. Steele Murdoch didn't even look at his watch. He merely smiled down at her, the smile conveying neither warmth nor greeting, she thought. Only politeness.

'No great hassle, I suppose,' he replied finally. 'I made our booking fairly vague, just in case.'

'Because you *expected* me to be late,' she accused, angry now at allowing that to happen, angrier that he'd obviously decided where they should eat without even asking her. And how had he managed that? she wondered. For a first-time visitor it would have taken hours to check out all the possibilities even with the detailed guides provided at the enormous shopping complex. She had a momentary vision then of Steele Murdoch whizzing round the place on one of the little rental scooters, and her anger faded into laughter at the thought. It was just *too* ridiculous.

'Because I wasn't entirely sure you'd show up at all,' he said, surprising in his candour—then softened the blow by adding, 'Not to mention how easy it would be to miss each other entirely in this place.'

'I didn't have any trouble finding *you*,' Anne replied, still defensive.

'Ah, but you live here. I'm just a tourist,' Steele responded with a false grin. 'You'd have to expect *me* to get lost.'

'Not likely,' she snapped. It was a ludicrous suggestion and well he knew it. Steele Murdoch wasn't the type to get lost anywhere.

Unbidden, one of his comments on the subject— made during a dinner at her father's farm—came to mind.

'I've never been lost in the bush,' he'd said. 'I lost my car once for three days, but——' Then he'd added, after patiently enduring hoots of derision, 'No, no, I knew exactly where *I* was; it was the car that was lost, along with the road home, of course. It wasn't a terribly intelligent car, that one; I traded it in not long afterwards.'

Anne shrugged off the memory and glared up at him, no longer sure she should have come, no longer sure of anything at all. He didn't seem intimidated, not that she ought to have expected him to be. 'Are you going to be shirty all evening?' he asked calmly. 'Where's your Christmas spirit, girl? Where's your sense of responsibility to your city? Here I am, a poor lonely, lost tourist, bewildered by this astonishing monument to the almighty dollar, and you can't even *try* to be nice?'

'I'm not in the tourism business,' Anne retorted, stung by the accusation despite the truth of it. Steele's flippant manner didn't help either. Didn't the man realise how traumatic he'd made things by just turning up out of the blue? Had he no idea of the feelings involved . . . the raw wounds he'd re-opened?

Clearly not. 'Well, you'd best get this acid out of your system now,' he said with a rueful shake of his head. 'It's not good for your digestion, and I can't see myself wasting good tucker on you if you're going to insist on behaving like a child.'

'I am not!' But she was, and she knew they both knew it.

'There's sure to be a McDonald's somewhere about,' he said, oblivious to her foul temper. 'They cater pretty well for ankle-biters, I understand.'

Anne stamped one dainty foot, but then, wisely, she thought, said nothing. It would only encourage him.

'Mind you,' he continued, 'you don't *look* like a child.' And now his eyes roved over her from crown to toe, and there was a new expression in them, an expression that held no banter, no sense of humour. This expression was one of almost possessive assessment. He was looking at her, through her, touching her with his eyes, his very touch disinterring memories best left buried.

She shivered inside, but forced herself to ignore the lust, the implied intimacy in that look. 'Child or not,' she said firmly, 'I'm starving; so whether it's to be posh tucker or a hamburger, let's get to it.'

'Your wish,' he replied, 'is my command.' It was a reply Anne would have loved ... if she could have believed it.

CHAPTER TWO

THE problem with Steele Murdoch wasn't that he lied; to Anne's knowledge he never did lie. It was just that he was so damnably devious, so utterly complex. As they moved slowly through the crowded shopping mall, she was all too conscious of his presence, his touch, and *their* beginning . . .

Like an old, old movie, their first meeting reeled through Anne's memory, spooling soundlessly at first, only to gather noise as her fear had been fuelled by noise at the time. Now she could put it all down to a combination of simple ignorance and indisputable jet-lag; at the time her reactions had been stamped blindly by panic at first, then by a degree of embarrassment she had never before experienced in the entire twenty-three years of her life.

'Australia—day 2; How I made a complete and total ass of myself without even trying.' If Anne had been the type to keep a diary, she thought, that would have been a suitably innocuous entry. At the very least, it would have been less revealing than a proper, detailed account.

It had begun so innocently too. There she was, less than forty-eight hours after arriving in Australia to be greeted by a father she hadn't seen since she was five years old but would have recognised anywhere, they looked so much alike, and the reunion—such as it was—was shaping up to be a total, utter disaster.

29

And it hadn't been her fault! Or, at least, not entirely. Not even mostly, she recalled. What was wrong wasn't so easily brought to account as that.

Until she'd actually stepped down from the aircraft, had allowed herself to be gathered into an embrace that was more polite than affectionate—on both sides—Anne hadn't realised how thoroughly she'd been conditioned to hate the man who had fathered her.

Her mother had hated Curtis Dunne; hated him with a passion beyond all logic, all reason. And, very likely, with just cause. But Anne had felt herself sufficiently removed from her father's leavetaking that she could face him without specific rancour.

That, of course, was before they met. Perhaps *met* wasn't quite the appropriate word, she'd thought during the lengthy plane trip from Edmonton to Vancouver to Honolulu to Sydney and eventually on to Hobart, a trip that now seemed more memorable for its return leg than it had at the beginning of her journey of discovery.

But it had been a meeting, rather than a reunion. Despite the ease of physical recognition, her father was a stranger to Anne, and she to him. Now, facing her third Christmas since that meeting, she half wished they'd stayed strangers.

In her saner moments, she realised that the strangeness wasn't the problem and hadn't been. The problem had been—and her father's stunningly beautiful wife Monique had been quick to notice and point it out—that despite being strangers they were simply too, too much alike!

'I'll have to change the seating,' Monique Dunne had said after their fourth meal together. 'I feel like some sort of novel, tucked between two bookends.'

That, of course, had been after Anne's traumatic, tragic, stupidly childish first meeting with Steele Murdoch, and while the remark had registered, had indeed become branded in her recall, at the time it had seemed insignificant.

Retrospect explained it all through jet-lag and stress; at the time it had simply been a case of too much, too fast, and yet also too little. Whatever emotional reaction she had expected from her father, and she couldn't honestly remember any such, what she got wasn't it!

He had been, right from the start, just as self-contained, just as cautious, just as outwardly prickly as she herself. Guilt, even diluted by nearly twenty years, was a powerful influence. She could see that now, even if she couldn't accept it.

Anne's parents had split up when she was five and her older sister was seven. It hadn't been an easy separation; indeed, sparse memory could recall horrendous screaming matches, vicious taunts and vindictiveness that even today could hardly be imagined.

There had been, of course, another woman. According to Anne's mother, many other women. Over many years; indeed, virtually throughout the years of the marriage prompted by her sister's conception, she had been told—and told *ad nauseam*.

She'd met the other woman once after the divorce and her father's remarriage, but her memories of the occasion were like smoke. Far more vivid was the recall of the vitriol her mother had spewed forth, the screaming and keening and the pure, naked hatred. She had a vague memory of her mother following them, driving recklessly—or so he said—as her father drove them to a city hotel for that single, fruitless visit. A memory of acid words and bitterness and anger and the rank taste of fear, yet mingled with ice-cream and cake and fizzy soft drinks.

He hadn't brought the other woman again, and not long after had moved to a town three hundred miles away. Visits had ceased then, and the girls had been told it was because he didn't care, never had and never would.

With adulthood, Anne wasn't so sure, but her childhood memories weren't sufficient to support any conclusion. Her father had hardly ever been home when he lived there; his work as a roving journalist had kept him on the move for weeks at a time; he had seemed only to come home to rest up for the next bout of wandering.

So after their meeting at the Hobart airport, after the first day of uncertainty and weariness and a horrid feeling of having made a mistake in coming at all, Anne had been only too happy to cut short the tension by going off for a walk by herself, pleading a wish to find her own first impressions of her father's so-called farm.

'Just watch out for the snakes,' she'd been warned. 'There's nothing else out there that'll hurt you; just mind where you put your feet.'

Easy advice, and sufficient, she'd thought at the time. But that was while she was still in sight of the house, before her trek up the narrow gravel road leading past had brought her to an enticing bush track and thence to another, and finally to a twilight that slid behind Mount Dromedary—her father's own personal mountain, he said—and brought the bush alive with sounds both familiar and frightening.

The maniacal, deranged laughter of the kookaburras had been more astonishing than frightening, deafeningly without direction but familiar enough from a host of jungly movies. Still, she'd turned about then and started heading back in what she'd thought was the right direction.

Then the black jays—the clinking currawongs—erupted from a copse of thick timber just ahead. Startled, Anne quickened her pace, only to slow it and finally stop in growing terror as a far more ominous sound rumbled from the scrub beside the track.

She felt her hackles rise, quivered to an enormity of terror that now seemed laughable. At the time it was anything but! The growls and snuffling in the darkening bush seemed straight from a horror movie, and in the stillness of the twilight became louder than life, more ominous than her imagination could stand. Anne quickened her pace at the first growl, was trotting by the third and running headlong towards the main road before she suddenly realised the sound was right beside her. Then it was panic stations all round, and she hit the gravel in a flying turn that destroyed her balance and sent her floundering with a shriek of terror towards the shoulder of the road and the tangled brush beyond.

The shape she saw then, lumbering along the verge towards her, was more than enough to triple her panic. Nothing in her admittedly meagre readings about Australia had prepared her for this! The chuffling, growling, evil gutturals seemed to surround her as she plunged face-first into the claws of some thorny bush,

and her shriek choked into a moan as she felt her
hands connect with what could only be a snake.

But it was no snake that caught the back of her
shirt in a single, reefing gesture that had her upright
and back on the road before the moan was ended.
Nor was it a snake that murmured, 'Steady on, little
mate,' as hands—very definitely hands, masculine
hands—clamped on her upper arms before she could
collapse into her terror. 'Steady on,' the voice repeated, louder this time and more forceful. 'There's
nothing to be afraid of, so stop panicking and give
yourself a chance to breathe.'

No snake, but the voice had a sibilance that was
equally frightening. To a city girl, the brush at twilight was bad enough; the noises she'd heard and what
she'd seen was too much, and to be grabbed by a
strange man was terror personified!

Anne's first reaction was to stay stock-still. That
lasted only an instant; then she was writhing against
his grip, kicking desperately with her knee towards his
most vulnerable parts and trying to stamp on his instep
at the same time. His muffled curse didn't stop her
assault of defence; it was the sudden resumption of
that horrid sound from the scrub beside them that did
that, and Anne's involuntary reaction was to stop
writhing and start screaming.

'Settle down, dammit!' Her attacker's lips were
close against her ear as he growled; she could feel the
warmth of his breath against her neck. She kicked out
once more, drew breath to scream, only to have one
arm released and the man's hand pressed tightly
against her lips.

'You're all right. Nothing's going to hurt you,'
droned the voice. 'Now I'm going to let you go and

try and put some light on the situation—but not if you're going to persist in trying to make me a soprano.'

He wasn't pleading, but the voice now held some element of reassurance. When he added, 'OK?' Anne, trembling, nodded her agreement. The hand was removed from her mouth, but he kept his grip on her arm as he fumbled briefly at his belt before turning on a torch and flashing it briefly across his own features.

'See, I'm just human,' he remarked. 'Now, having got that squared away, maybe you'd fancy telling me just what the hell's got you so spooked. Not afraid of the dark, by any chance?'

Anne shivered, still very afraid—and not of the dark!—despite his assurances. Before she could speak, the harsh growling screams erupted again, and she flinched away from the sound, looking to the dark shadow beside her, darker now that the torch had been turned off.

'I...no, not the dark,' she stammered, then flinched again as the growling was repeated. 'Wh—what *is* that?'

His first response was a soft, almost gentle chuckle, a rumbling that grew in texture as he turned partly away from her as if only now aware of the noise. 'That? Just devils fighting over a road kill or a bit of rubbish somebody's dumped.'

'Devils?' she asked, now thoroughly confused. What on earth was he talking about? 'But I saw...I saw a bear.'

Then he laughed openly, though still very softly. 'You'll be Curtis Dunne's girl, obviously.' And he chuckled again. 'You saw a what?'

'A *bear*!' she insisted. 'And stop laughing at me, damn it. I know what a bear looks like.'

'So,' he said with hardly a break in his chuckling, 'do I. And whatever it was you saw, dear girl, it was not a bear and it was not dangerous. I can assure you of that.'

'Well, it *looked* dangerous,' she retorted sharply, anger now rising to overshadow her fears. This man, whoever he was, obviously wasn't afraid, and the fact that he seemed to know who she was must count for something.

His face—so briefly revealed in the torch beam—remained imprinted in her mind, strongly chiselled, with the features set off by the inky hair and eyebrows. It was a face that could have been etched from the stone of this oldest continent on earth. Deep-set eyes, probably as black as his hair, had brushed across her face with the same lightness as the laughter that met her remark.

Laughter... then a sudden silence that was as suddenly punctuated by a high-pitched, snuffling grunt now ahead of them.

'Ah,' he said, 'now I know what you're on about. Come and we'll have a look, with a bit of luck.' The command was aided by a fierce grip on her wrist. Anne had to follow whether she willed it or no. Her light shoes felt decidedly flimsy as she stumbled in the wake of this dark figure that plunged quickly but silently down the shadowy road ahead of them. She tried to gasp out her objection to being dragged along like a sack of potatoes, but her objection got only a muted shush and a rude jerk on her wrist.

They walked for what seemed like aeons but was probably only a moment; then the shadow halted and

Anne stumbled into his back as he freed her hand to reach once more for his torch.

'Ready?'

The question was filled with an almost childish excitement, and her whispered, 'Yes,' was caught up in the mood.

'Right—here's your bear!'

The torchlight spun a pool of light ahead of them to where a squat, rotund figure waddled round in a clumsy turn to stare with piggy eyes at the light. Anne could only stare. The thing was nearly the size of a small pig, but it looked more to her like an overgrown beaver, or some similar rodent.

'Badger,' her guide whispered as if in reply to her unspoken question. Anne choked down an angry rejection, and just in time. 'It's not, of course,' the man continued. 'There's no such thing in Australia, but that's what the locals here call it—actually, it's a wombat.'

'Wombat,' she repeated parrot-like, wondering at the sanity of it all.

'I expect the original settlers called it that because it lives in a burrow like the European badger,' the man said, speaking patiently, as she herself did when explaining something to a particularly slow child. 'You're lucky to be hearing so much racket off this lad; usually they're pretty quiet.'

'Is all this somehow significant?' Anne asked, then reared back with a start as the animal grunted and snuffled and rollicked towards them.

'Only to him, I expect,' was the reply from her unmoving companion. 'This one's been a pet at some time, and it'll be the death of him one day if he doesn't learn that all people aren't friendly. Go on . . . get out of it,' he shouted then, stamping his foot and advancing on the creature with enormous ferocity. The animal turned tail immediately and scuttled for the cover of the adjoining bush, but not without a final whuffle of indignation at the rebuff.

'That wasn't very nice,' said Anne, fears forgotten as she immediately took the animal's side in the clearly unequal contest.

'It wasn't meant to be,' was the stern reply. 'As I said, he's got to learn that people aren't all friendly. That, or stay the hell off the roads where he could get run over or shot. He lives up in the corner of my top paddock, usually, and he's safe enough there, but occasionally he decides to go walkabout, and this is the result.'

He paused then, staring down at her in silence. He was, Anne reckoned, about five feet ten, certainly tall enough to tower over her diminutive five feet two. And, though his face was in shadow, she suddenly realised that her own was not. While he'd been explaining about the wandering wombat, a full moon had peeped over a distant ridge to flood the bush night with silvery light.

'There goes any chance of showing you the devils,' he said. 'The torch won't hold them in this light. They've gone quiet, which likely means gone entirely. I expect you frightened them off with all your carrying on. Our little mate Willy the Wombat would have done the same, if he weren't half-tame.

'You'd best give your face a wipe,' he said then, hauling a handkerchief from his trouser pocket. But even as she reached for it he changed his mind, and reached out to pull her closer to him as he started to do the job himself.

'Do you *mind*?' Anne snarled, pulling away from him and grabbing the hanky from his fingers as she did so. 'I'm quite capable of wiping my own face, for goodness' sake.'

His response was a display of gleaming teeth in a grin that only widened as she touched on a scratch and winced with the sudden sharp pain.

'Should have let me do it,' he said reflectively, and then, with startling perceptiveness, 'What are you doing out by yourself anyway? Familial visit soured already?'

Anne gasped at his accuracy. 'Soured' mightn't be quite the right word, but certainly she had sought her own company in a bid to try and come to terms with the feeling that her journey to Australia had been one gigantic mistake.

Not that she'd give this stranger the satisfaction of knowing that! 'I'd think it's a bit early to be making judgements like that,' she replied testily. 'I've only been here——'

'Almost two days,' he interrupted. 'And instead of being at home trying to get to know your father better, here you are wandering round the scrub like a lost sheep.'

'I was taking a walk! Is that a crime or something?'

He shrugged shoulders so broad that they stretched the fabric of his T-shirt. 'Making people worry isn't either; but it's hardly what I'd call polite, so tuck your shirt in and we'll trundle down and see if they've still got the coffee-pot on.'

Only then did Anne realise that in his pulling her from the thicket he'd come dangerously close to disrobing her in the process. Her shirt was hanging loose at the back, and had pulled free halfway down the front as well.

She turned away to fasten it, totally unamused by his callous chuckle. 'I'm quite capable of finding my own way back,' she argued over her shoulder. 'More than capable, in fact.'

'Oh, I don't doubt it for a minute,' he replied. 'And I'm quite capable of making my own coffee, but your stepmother does it better, and puts out biccies as well.'

Stepmother! It was a word Anne detested, and a fact that only complicated everything she was trying to come to terms with. The woman for whom her family had been abandoned was only a shadow in memory; Monique Dunne was an all-too-vivid reality.

Not much taller than Anne, and substantially younger than her husband, she had every hallmark of the stereotypical wicked stepmother, and yet none, for what sense it made. She was beautiful, with honey-blonde hair of a thickness and lustre Anne would have killed for, ice-green, slightly hooded eyes, and that lilting, faint French accent that was either too good to be true or too true to be good.

What on earth was she doing married to a pudgy, not very tall and greying middle-aged man like Anne's father?

Another thing difficult to come to terms with. Anne's memory was of a *young* man, a laughing, kindly, loving man, the little she and her sister had seen of him, cross on occasion with their mother, but seldom with them. The man who had met her at the airport had been a shock.

Years of riotous living, or so she presumed, had clearly taken their toll. Curtis Dunne was only in his late forties, but looked ten years older. His face was lined and tired-looking, he had huge bags under his eyes, and a generally unhealthy tone overall. But the genetic resemblance was there, so strong that it had also shocked her. She was this man's daughter, and so much like him that if she was attractive—as she was often told—then he must have been too... once. It was like coming face to face with herself grown old and dissolute.

'Sure no question of the relationship, anyway. You're the spitting image of the old fellow.' The stranger might have been reading her mind, and that, for some reason, only served to increase her defensiveness, and on her father's part as well.

'Hardly old,' she argued, reversing her own feelings on exactly that subject. 'Not that much older than you, I would have thought.'

An outright lie! This man was still in his early thirties, no more than ten years older than herself, Anne guessed. And what did it matter anyway? Except that his attitude made her see red without half trying.

His laugh, as he stepped out along the road, was infectious, or could have been in different circumstances. Now it was merely offensive.

'I'm a veritable child by comparison, just like you,' he chuckled. 'Well, maybe not quite like you, since I'm not young enough to be his son unless he got an earlier start than he admits to.'

Anne, stepping out to try and match the man's long strides, wondered just how old that was. Her father had been only eighteen when her parents were married.

'He'd have had to be thirteen, if that helps your sums any,' the stranger said with a moonlit grin, a mocking grin that added to her frustration. 'Not impossible, I suppose, but hardly likely.'

Anne was having too much trouble keeping up to bother replying. And now the stranger, as if finally noticing, slowed his pace to match her own.

'I hope you'll give the old fellow a chance,' he said then, with what appeared to be genuine concern in his voice. 'I know it's difficult for you, after all this time, but it's probably worse for him, you know, all things considered.'

'And you're some kind of expert, I suppose,' Anne replied, not bothering to hide her bitterness. 'How many children have you left abandoned in your travels?'

'Not a single one that I'm aware of,' he responded with infuriating calm. 'And if you're carrying a grudge for the problems he and your mother had when you were just a child, why did you bother coming here in the first place? You're mature enough, surely, to realise that kind of thing could only be self-defeating.'

'Maybe I get turned on by revenge,' Anne had retorted with a sneer. How dared this man—whoever he was—start to question her motives? Not that she was all that sure of them herself, but that was beside the point. It was decidedly none of his business.

'Oh, I doubt that,' he said after a moment. 'Or, at least, I hope not, let's put it that way. If you're as vindictive as all that, it's going to make for a pretty rough summer all round.'

'Well, I don't know what that has to do with you,' she snapped. 'It's my summer, and my father, after all.'

'Your father; my friend,' was the blunt reply. 'And since I reckon I've known him longer than you have and a good deal better besides, *and* he's my neighbour, it might turn out to have plenty to do with me.'

Neighbour? Well, she realised, of course he must be a neighbour; he'd hardly be walking down this road if he didn't live somewhere reasonably close. Memory stirred then, and a name popped into her mind and on to her tongue at the same instant.

'Murdoch ... Steele Murdoch,' she said, speaking to herself as she tried to put the half-remembered name to the moonlit features of her companion. Her father had mentioned him in one or two of the letters they'd exchanged prior to Anne's visit, but only now did the name come to mind.

'The very same,' he agreed in calm tones, the reply unexpected until Anne realised she had spoken aloud. 'I'm surprised, though, that it's a name you'd re-member. Your father must have said something nice about me.'

'I've yet to hear him say anything nasty about anybody,' she said. True enough; they'd hardly had the chance to become involved in discussions of such depth.

'He seldom does,' Steele Murdoch said quietly. 'You'll find he's usually able to find a good word about almost anybody.'

'Except my mother,' Anne muttered bitterly, speaking as much to herself as to Steele Murdoch.

'Well, that's a subject we've not discussed too often,' was the reply. 'But I've always had the im-pression he thought most of the blame for their splitting up was his.'

'It sounds to me as if you've talked about it more than you're admitting,' Anne said, then went ab-ruptly silent. It was ludicrous, she thought, to be dis-cussing something so intimate as her parents' marital difficulties with a total stranger!

He merely shrugged. 'Maybe so,' he admitted. 'And of course it's none of my business anyway. But I think you've come here looking for answers that may not exist, if not for the vengeance you've mentioned, and I'd hate to see you so blinded by the past that you can't see the future.'

'Just what I need, a moonlight philosopher,' she sneered. 'Well, I hate to disappoint you, Mr Murdoch, but you know very little about my past, and my future is my own affair.'

'I know the past is done and finished and nothing any of us can do will change it,' he replied. 'And as for the future—well . . .'

He walked along in silence, stopping only when they came in sight of the farmhouse lights ahead. 'I know you think I'm interfering,' he said then, 'but just to satisfy my chauvinistic curiosity, why *did* you come here? It must have been a difficult decision, all things considered.'

The politeness of the question threw Anne off-balance, but not as much as her inability to formulate a rational reply. She'd been asking herself much the same question ever since a minor lottery win had provided the funds and some inner feeling had matched it with an impromptu decision.

Her mother's response had been predictably hostile; she had indeed, at first, refused to even provide Anne with Curtis Dunne's address. Several weeks of slanging matches and the quite outrageous emotional blackmail in which her mother specialised had served only to harden Anne's resolve to make the visit, but determination was quite a different thing from reasoned consideration. Even having arrived in Australia, even having met her father, she was no closer to knowing just why she'd made the journey in the first place.

'Curiosity, I suppose,' she finally said, looking up to meet Steele Murdoch's gaze in the dazzling moonlight. The frankness of his question had set aside her defences for the moment, and she tried to answer him fairly. 'I . . . I really can't be clearer than that,' she added. 'I don't know just what I expected to find, or . . . or . . . whatever.'

'And whatever it was, that's not what you found, I presume,' he said with discerning insight. 'Well, it's early days yet; I wouldn't get my knickers in a knot over it yet if I were you.' And then he grinned, teeth gleaming in the moonlight, and reached out to take her hand and give it a single quick squeeze. 'So let's leave it for now and go see if the coffee-pot's still on, shall we?'

He didn't even wait for a reply before leading her down the driveway and knocking loudly at the kitchen door. 'I found this stray lamb wandering along the road,' he announced, walking into the house without waiting for his knock to be answered. 'It's a bit skinny, but I thought you'd probably want it back.'

Curtis Dunne merely grinned a welcome as he turned in his chair. His wife Monique was far more forthcoming.

'Steele! Trust you to turn up as soon as there's a pretty girl on the place. I thought you were in Sydney, or New Zealand or somewhere.' She crossed the kitchen with a feline grace and leaned up to collect Steele Murdoch's kiss with—Anne thought—a great deal of enthusiasm.

'*Two* pretty girls,' he corrected after the kiss. 'Although this one hasn't kissed me yet.' And, to

Anne's dismay, he looked at her as if expecting her to remedy that shortcoming immediately. 'And she should have, too, considering that I rescued her from the clutches of some howling devils and a ravenous wombat. That's why she's so grotty; she tried to run and tripped into a patch of ferns.'

Monique squealed with laughter and immediately demanded to hear the entire saga in detail. Anne took the opportunity to flee to the bathroom, where the mirror confirmed Steele's 'grotty' description. She took some time to tidy herself up, all the while hearing his low, rumbling voice and her stepmother's peals of seductive laughter as the lot of them enjoyed her discomfort.

It took all her nerve just to return to the kitchen, where a cup of coffee was immediately thrust into her hand. 'You probably need this,' Monique said with a smile. 'It must have been terrifying for you. And I'm sure this one——' with a coquettish glance towards Steele Murdoch '—was no help at all. He'd have laughed; he's a very devil himself.'

'Only a chuckle,' Steele interjected. 'I'm not a sadist, after all.'

'You're worse than that,' smiled the blonde Monique. 'We would have locked Anne up if we'd known you were back. You're not to be trusted with pretty girls around.'

In the light, his broad grin wasn't quite so wolfish, but the gleam in his eye when he looked at Anne held deep lights that hadn't been so obvious in the moonlight. He raised one sooty eyebrow as his mouth quirked around the grin. 'I'd be less than fair if I didn't admit that,' he said, and his eyes locked with

Anne's as he spoke. 'But then I didn't realise she was quite so pretty. The light, after all, was pretty dim.'

Anne said nothing. She sipped at her coffee, using the opportunity to take a good long look at her rescuer. The moonlight, she decided, had flattered him. In clear light, his face was too ruggedly lean, too sharp-edged and harsh with total masculinity. Except when he grinned, of course. Smiling, he was quite attractive, and she knew she wasn't the first woman to see it.

A glance towards her stepmother confirmed that hypothesis; Monique Dunne clearly fancied Steele Murdoch's raffish good looks, and Anne wondered just how much she fancied them. The two of them certainly seemed very close. Anne wondered then if her father was getting some of his own back, and felt a brief surge of... *something*, at the thought.

Her stepmother, she quickly determined, was a born flirt. But there was more to it than just that where Steele Murdoch was concerned, she was certain. It seemed that everything Monique said to him contained some hidden, secret meaning, that every time she looked at him her hooded eyes laughed secretly.

The feeling continued throughout the evening, although Anne was often confused by her own reactions to the tall, slender, ebony-haired Steele Murdoch. The Steele Murdoch whose gaze varied between a deliberate undressing of her and something so different, so remote that it made her feel quite... childish.

Because Anne was so uncertain of her place in her father's house, of her personal reaction to each individual person there, she tried to say little, to let *them* make the running. But it was hard; both Steele and Monique were experts, it seemed, at drawing out such shyness, at making the stranger feel comfortable in spite of herself. Without realising it, Anne would suddenly find herself talking a mile a minute, and would catch herself, shift gears back into her shyness, her uncertainty.

Her father seemed content to let Monique and Steele do all this; he contributed little to the easy, if erratic drift of the conversation, seeming to have accepted that he and Anne could almost communicate without words, they thought so much alike.

And Steele, too, seemed prone to that habit. When Monique was carrying the conversation he swung his attention between her and Anne, and his attention was occasionally so intense as to be nearly frightening. He seemed able to read her like a book, and his own expression wasn't much more difficult to interpret. When Anne's comments were such as he approved, there was a glitter of almost sexual excitement in those deep dark eyes. But when she began to blather, to slip into areas he obviously considered childish, his eyes would change, harden, lose interest. She found even that first evening that she had a compulsive urge to please him.

With her father and stepmother he was totally comfortable, almost to the point of treating their home as his own. Clearly the three of them were old and valued friends, except for the moments when Anne was convinced there was more than that between her stepmother and her own dark-haired rescuer.

Steele Murdoch the black knight, rescuer of fair maidens, champion of damsels in distress. No white knight, not ever. Not this rugged man with his military bearing and his fathomless, changeable boardroom-bedroom eyes.

And yet, even in the beginning, there had been a quality of gentleness about him that Anne, now struggling to match his pace through the milling throngs of the West Edmonton Mall, realised she had never doubted, not even when he'd rejected her, not even when—although—she hated him for it.

She *had* been too young for him then, might still be too young for him now. Wouldn't be, she thought, if only Steele himself weren't so complex, so... together. Never a doubt, not for him. He was what he was, knew what he wanted, and didn't—hadn't—wanted her.

Which didn't make this evening any easier to understand, not least because she knew, instinctively, that he was going out of his way to make sure it was difficult for her to understand. He was a man too much in control, dangerous, not safe like her own predictable, comfortable John. Just how much in control, just how truly manipulative, she realised when she discovered their destination.

CHAPTER THREE

IT WAS no great surprise, really, for Anne to be led into the nearby Fantasyland Hotel's very upmarket Fantasy Dining-Room, though she *did* wonder just a bit at Steele's choice. But not for long.

'I suppose you might have preferred one of the livelier places,' Steele said as they entered, 'but I like to be able to hear myself think when I'm talking to somebody.'

'Your choice,' she murmured, then went quiet as the head waiter arrived, greeting Steele by name and leading them to their table with a degree of obsequiousness that would have been funny if it hadn't been so in keeping with the entire ambience of the dining-room.

I'd hate to see what you call *really* posh, Anne thought as they were seated at a table glittering with silver service. Not, of course, before her coat had been taken, handled like mink instead of the well-worn sheepskin it really was.

She declined a drink. 'It's risky enough driving at night in the winter, and at this time of year...'

'A wise decision, although I think you might make an exception and have at least one glass of wine with dinner,' Steele replied, his grin now openly friendly but his eyes still appraising Anne as if he was trying to read her mind. 'They managed to find me a reasonable drop of Australian wine—thank heaven.

Some of the stuff you people drink here and call good wines is quite astonishing.'

He seemed nonplussed by her request that *he* do the ordering of the meal, pausing only to enquire— still with that suspicious, open grin—if she was 'peckish, proper hungry, or what?'

'If "what" means ravenous, there's your answer,' she replied boldly. 'I haven't eaten anywhere this posh since I got home, and I warn you that I intend to take every advantage.'

'I wish you would,' said Steele, and his eyes twinkled as Anne flushed on realising his not-so-hidden meaning. But she said nothing, only looked away, forcing herself to gaze round the luxurious dining-room as she fought to collect herself, fought for the strength to meet his approaches without giving in. *Very* posh, she thought. Bordering indeed upon very, *very*.

He didn't push, merely outwaited her, knowing she would have to turn and meet his triumphant grin sooner or later. It was a tactic that would have been more effective without the intrusion of the waitress, and Anne bubbled at having scored one success at least.

Steele ignored her pleasure while he went through the menu and discussed various possibilities before settling on choices that proved his memory of her taste in food.

One for you, she thought, but kept silent, determined now to wait him out, to make him break the growing silence by—with any luck—explaining his presence in Canada and more importantly his presence again in her life.

It was a long wait, one in which Anne's nervousness could only increase in direct proportion to her frustration. She filled it by fighting the urge to scream or throw something at him; he just undressed her with his eyes and probed at memories she didn't want released. And when he did finally speak it was such a deliberate, contrived production that she almost laughed.

'Your father's as well as can be expected; your stepmother's as lovely and scatter-brained as ever; there hasn't been a serious bush-fire since you left and they still only grade the road just before the rates notices come out,' he said, and then continued through a litany of utter trivia that became more and more totally irrelevant as he rambled on...and on...and...

'You didn't come here to feed me that load of rubbish,' Anne finally said, glaring at him across the expanse of silver cutlery, but keeping her voice low, her attitude reasonable.

'No, I suppose I didn't,' he replied with equal calm. But whatever he might have added was forestalled by the arrival of their first course, delivered by a waitress whose very professional attitude was clearly touched by a quite unprofessional interest in Anne's companion. Her appreciation went unremarked, but to the fury of an unexpected jealousy which had Anne seething. What was it, she wondered, that seemed to prompt women to not only find Steele Murdoch attractive, but to make dead certain he knew it?

Well, not me, mate, she told him silently, lapsing into Australianisms as she often did when the more sedate Canadianisms proved wanting. It was, she had often thought, a delightful language when you wanted to call a spade something more colourful than just a shovel. I've had you right up to *here* and now I'm immune. It was a splendid stand, even if she didn't quite believe it herself.

During the meal, Steele confined his comments to more or less conventional social chit-chat, asking Anne about her work, about the city of Edmonton, and about the vast playground of the West Edmonton Mall, which was the primary purpose, he said, of his visit to Canada.

'I've got a consortium that's vaguely looking at something similar,' he said, 'so I took the opportunity to come and have a look for myself.'

Anne couldn't help laughing. 'Something similar to this in *Hobart*? That's ridiculous. You could put the whole of downtown Hobart inside this place and still have room for the Water Park and damned near every other shop in Tasmania.'

'Who said anything about Hobart?' Steele countered. 'There's more to Australia than just Hobart, although I will concede Tasmania is far and away the best part.'

'You're as bad as my father,' Anne replied with a scowl of dismay. 'He thinks it's the centre of the universe—won't even visit the mainland if he can get out of it.'

'Much less make a return visit to Canada,' Steele added perceptively. 'But then you must understand that he made that transition without knowing he still had any ties in Canada. It makes a difference.'

'It doesn't even make sense, much less a difference,' Anne retorted. 'How can you say he didn't know he had any ties? What are my sister and I, not to mention her children, if not ties?'

Steele's eyes had turned serious, and he deliberately waited until the dessert had been served and the waitress was out of earshot before he answered her challenge.

'At the time he came to Tasmania, I rather think both you and your sister were hardly more than memories of children he'd given up for the sake of their future happiness,' he said then.

'Given up? *Abandoned* is more like it,' Anne snapped, her voice hard despite the tempting dessert in front of her.

'That's your outlook on the situation, and hardly surprising,' Steele replied calmly, ignoring her attitude as he dug into his lemon meringue pie.

'It's not my attitude—it's the fact of the matter,' Anne insisted. Her own pie no longer appeared so appetising as old wounds were reopened.

'From *your* viewpoint, and logically, I presume, from your mother's,' was the gentle, ever-so-calm reply. 'Your father, of course, looked at the matter quite differently. Not that I should have to try and explain any of this to you, since he's already done so.'

'Not an explanation,' Anne insisted stubbornly. 'Excuses, that's all.'

'Excuses in a sense, yes,' he answered. 'Your father's not a complete fool; he knew how you'd feel about the whole situation. Although,' he added without a smile, 'I very much doubt if he expected your sense of vindictiveness to be quite so well developed.'

'It isn't being vindictive to face up to the fact of having been abandoned,' Anne said. 'And that's what he did—no matter how *you* might try and twist things to fit your typically chauvinistic impressions and attitudes.'

Her barbed remarks bounced off without a sign of scoring a hit; Steele Murdoch was impervious to her anger, to her sense of moral outrage at her father's actions of so many years ago.

'So indignant . . . so positive of your rightness,' he finally said, again without smiling but with eyes that radiated something approaching sadness. 'I'd feel sorry for you if all this self-righteousness was accomplishing anything—but it isn't. It's just made you all bitter and twisted and destroyed whatever chance you might have had of making things up with your father before . . . well . . .'

'Before what?' Anne wasn't certain he'd deliberately let his remark falter, and even if he had it was too tempting a bait to ignore.

But now, to her smouldering anger, he shrugged off the demand. 'Hardly matters, does it?' he said. 'You're here and he's in Tasmania, and there isn't a helluva lot of communication between the two of you.'

'None of which,' she insisted, 'is any of your damned business in the first place.'

'As you've repeated *ad nauseam*,' Steele said. 'Why don't you finish your dessert instead of repeating yourself?'

Anne looked down at her pie, then immediately back up to where his dark eyes were busy appraising her reaction. 'You're really a bit of a bastard, you know,' she said, then picked up her fork and turned her concentration upon the splendid dessert.

'I've been told it often enough,' he growled, 'that if I didn't know better I might actually start to believe it. Which, I suspect, wouldn't impress my dear old mum; she'd be spinning in her grave just at the suggestion.'

'I didn't mean it that way, and what's more you know it,' Anne responded, manoeuvring the words around a mouthful of pie. '*Bastard*' was about the most common word in what passed for the English language in Australia, after 'bloody' and 'the', and well he knew it!

'Do I indeed?' he replied, and she immediately glared up at him, expecting that too familiar gleam of mockery in his eyes. But it wasn't there; instead there was a brief hint of something else . . . sadness?

'Yes,' she insisted. 'Yes, you do.'

'Whatever you say.' And now his expression had altered slightly. What she might have interpreted as sadness now seemed more like a bleak acceptance, a withdrawing of whatever tenuous thread of communication had been building between them. For some reason, Anne now felt guilty herself.

'It's not a matter of whatever I say,' she found herself snarling. 'It's a matter of . . . well . . . of what *is*, that's what!'

'And you, of course, know exactly what *is*, the whole of it?'

His features didn't reveal it, but she was sure there was a sneering, a mocking in his voice. Or did she just expect that?

'Well, I certainly know more about what's between my father and me than you do,' she said angrily. 'After all——'

'After all, he *is* your father and you *are* his daughter,' Steele broke in. 'And, after all, you've known each other all of . . . what . . . five and a half years out of the past twenty-five? And only six months of *that* face to face like real people. Oh, that's significant, that is.'

'Well, it's more significant than your damned smug attitude towards all this,' Anne flared. 'You ... you give me the pip, you and your know-it-all attitude.'

'I've known your father longer—and better, I suggest—than you,' he responded with unexpected quietness. 'And I'd even go so far as to suggest that I know you just a bit better than your father does, although admittedly not for quite so long.'

The assertion was uttered in a voice that was flat as winter moonlight, but it smashed through Anne's defences like a lash, flaying at her innermost feelings, adding fuel to her anger, to her guilt.

For what seemed like hours, she couldn't speak, could hardly think as shame ravaged her senses. And then, 'You arrogant so-and-so!' she hissed, and her narrowed eyes flashed fire as she threw down her napkin and started to force back her chair, to get up and get away from this man whose knowledge of her, whose ability to play upon her weaknesses, made her so totally vulnerable.

'Sit down.'

His voice still held that damnable calm, but there was nothing calm about the fingers that now laced around her wrist. He'd reached across the table so quickly that she'd not even seen the motion, but now his grip was like that of a manacle. She might be able to rise to her feet, but flee? Never! She glared across into eyes like soot, eyes that seemed fathomless, almost expressionless. But around those eyes all Steele Murdoch's features radiated a blistering anger that matched her own.

'Now!' he insisted. And Anne obeyed. It was only just within her capabilities to cause a scene here in such a smart restaurant, but she knew that Steele Murdoch had no such qualms, despite being a guest in the place. He would make a scene if it suited him to do so, and be damned to anyone who might dare to interfere.

She sat in stubborn silence, forcing herself to meet his eyes, gradually becoming aware that his grip on her wrist had altered, had become almost a caress. And she realised suddenly that to any casual onlooker it would appear just that—a man reaching across a dinner table with a gesture quite in keeping with the intimacy of a Christmas-season dinner for lovers.

She tensed, ready to wrench away her arm at the first opportunity, but a quirky grin at the corners of his generous mouth made it clear that he was way ahead of her.

'Now just settle down,' he said in a soft voice. 'This is no place for a war, not that we need have one anyway.'

'Please let me go.'

'Not until I'm satisfied you'll behave,' he said, and his voice was calmness itself. 'You are the most volatile woman I think I've ever run across.'

Volatile. Anne almost shivered at the word and the memories that it sent flashing through her mind. Steele's eyes, she found, were almost hypnotic, and his calm, steady gaze seemed to send her mind back in time, as did the warm touch of his now gentle fingers...

It had been that touch, she thought, more than anything else about him, that had led her to fall in love—no, to become *infatuated* with him!

Of course, there had been the attraction of his not quite conventional good looks, his masculinity, strength and obvious sense of character. But during the first part of her Australian experience, when she had been both at her most and least vulnerable, it had been his touch, his gentleness, that had taken her in.

After that first meeting, he'd turned up at her step-mother's table quite often. Too often, Anne had thought at first, her suspicious mind convinced on one day that Steele and Monique Dunne had a thriving affair on the go, yet equally convinced a day later that she was deluding herself.

Often, indeed, she'd wondered if she was only wishing such an affair as some sort of weird revenge upon her father. And yet . . . Steele had quite often taken Monique into the city with him, had quite often seemed—if only by chance—to meet Anne's father's wife for lunch, or for a drink. On the few occasions when Anne had been with Monique, it had all seemed to be by chance, but when she hadn't been along? Yet Monique had always mentioned such meetings when she returned, and Curtis Dunne would merely nod, or make a suitably appropriate comment.

Of course, Hobart was such a small city, Anne had often thought. Anyone frequenting the city centre could hardly help but run across friends, neighbours or acquaintances on a fairly regular basis.

For her father, she realised, it must be quite a different situation. He hardly ever went to town, hardly ever left his so-called farm, in fact. His days were spent either at the word processor or out playing at one of his hobbies.

'He's a loner,' Steele had said to her on one occasion. 'Not quite the loner he thinks he is—or thinks he'd like to be—but essentially that's what he is.'

'More like a mis...whatever,' she'd replied. 'He's just straight out antisocial, that's what.'

'The word is *misanthrope*, and he's not, really,' Steele had continued. 'His problem is just that he thinks too much, among other things. Most people don't, you know. Or at least they don't think of anything your old man considers terribly relevant. But he isn't antisocial, or at least no more than you are. Just...well...rather private.'

'I am *not* antisocial,' she had declared. 'Private...well, yes, to be honest, I suppose I am that. But definitely not antisocial. I quite like people.'

'And so does your father, provided he can deal with them on his own terms.'

'And in his own time, and at his own pleasure,' Anne had replied with a petulant sneer. 'He's the same with me. I don't know what the hell I'm doing here, most of the time. He doesn't talk to me, hardly knows I'm around.'

'Ah, you poor, neglected thing,' was the reply, but, to her delight/amazement/concern, Steele had gathered her into the crook of one arm and held her close against him, her head falling naturally into the hollow of his shoulder.

She had made no move to escape; indeed her first reaction had been to look up, to meet his eyes and see if they held some message less casual than the embrace she was so much enjoying.

Held in an invisible net cast from his sooty black eyes, she had found herself breathless and yet tingling with a strange excitement. For an instant she had thought he was going to kiss her, and the thought had made her both expectant and afraid.

She'd known so little of this man who had suddenly taken such a part in her new, if temporary existence. She'd fancied him something crazy, but all her instincts had told her it was too much, too soon. He was too old for her, too different in attitudes, in lifestyle, in . . . everything!

Becoming involved, she had thought at the time, would be little short of stupid. He was her father's friend, most likely her stepmother's lover, and, most important, he was far, far too much for Anne herself to handle.

This man, she knew, wouldn't be content with playing games dependent on sexual overtones. He wasn't like her own John, who was . . . well . . . manipulatable. John loved her, and of course that involved some element of sex, she supposed. But John could be handled, managed. He had nothing of this man's mature sexuality, none of his sheer, almost blatant masculinity. John was . . . safe.

'Your problem with your old man,' Steele had said then, severing her thoughts with an almost brutal pragmatism, 'is that you're too damned much alike.'

And with that telling remark he'd let Anne go. Indeed, he'd almost thrust her away. And if there had been any matching of her own lustful wanting he'd hidden it so well that she could only have imagined it.

Instead, over the next few weeks, he had put himself into the role of guide, rather than confidant. There was still that tenderness, though, even if he'd made no obvious attempt to get too close, to reveal any more than necessary of either his feelings or hers.

He hadn't kept himself at a distance, hadn't made any perceptible effort to keep from touching her, from being close to her. It was just...that somehow he *did*! It was like being shown a strange place by some older brother, Anne had thought at the time. She'd never had an older brother, of course, but in principle...

'You've lost a fair bit of weight since you left us.'

She returned to the present with a start, yanked from her reverie by his voice and just as quickly on guard because of some half-hidden tone therein.

Meeting his glance, she found his eyes just completing a far too thorough appraisal of her. Damn the man! When he looked at her like that, she might have been sitting naked before him, she thought, and immediately lowered her eyes lest he read the thoughts.

'Being a gay bachelor girl not all it's cracked up to be?' he continued, the insistence in his voice countered by the tiny light of laughter she could detect in his eyes if she would only dare look hard enough.

'Even in the wilds of Tasmania, people know better than to use the word "gay" so...non-specifically,' Anne replied with a faltering smile. 'And I'm not a bachelor girl either; the word is...'

'Spinster! Which is among the ugliest words in the English language,' Steele snapped. 'Don't play at semantics with me, little Miss Dunne. And least of all those involved with the so-called sexual revolution. You know what I'm getting at as well as I do.'

'Yes. And if you're implying that I'm a skinny, lesbian spinster, you can keep your opinion to yourself,' Anne snapped back at him. 'Unless of course you only brought me here to insult me.'

'I don't take women to dinner for that purpose,' was the studied reply. 'I usually do so for the sheer pleasure of their company.'

'For the pleasure of their company *after* dinner, more like it,' Anne snorted, for some reason now wanting to hit out, to attack. If she didn't, she knew, Steele Murdoch would only succeed in getting behind her guard once again, and it was just too painful, too hurtful.

He ought to have been offended, but he merely shrugged. 'You might have lost some weight, but your tongue's just as sharp as ever,' he muttered. 'I reckon it's all this vindictiveness that keeps you skinny. You should try being a bit more forgiving, a bit more tolerant.'

'I need all the tolerance I have for the children,' she replied, deliberately trying to enforce the distance between then. 'They, at least, deserve it.'

'So does your father!'

Anne nearly gasped her surprise at his bitterness, the icy harshness of the soft-spoken words. Steele's voice was so low it was barely audible even just across the table, but it was as if his voice were issuing from some dark, cold cave.

And then, before she could even think to reply, he was signalling for the bill, the iciness gone or at least overlaid by his normal veneer of civilisation.

The head-waiter was there in seconds, and Steele politely thanked him for the meal after signing the bill, then stalked silently round the table to take Anne by the arm.

'I think we'll look for somewhere a bit more...private for our nightcap, my dear,' he said with a meaningful glance at the obsequious head waiter, who smiled knowingly.

Anne could have kicked him, but was forestalled by the return of her sheepskin coat and the knowledge that Steele would almost certainly be expecting such a move, and would be more than prepared for it.

His grip on her arm never slackened as they left the dining-room and walked through to the hotel's spacious and well-appointed lobby.

'Liqueurs at my place, I think,' he said in a tone that warned her he would brook no argument on the suggestion.

Anne decided, however, that a token argument was the least defence she ought to put up; being alone with Steele Murdoch—especially somewhere as intimate as his hotel room—was to be avoided at any cost.

'No, thank you,' she replied, turning swiftly to try and free her arm from his grasp before he could direct her to the bank of lifts. 'I don't especially want anything more to drink.'

'You don't want to be alone with me, is what you mean,' he said calmly. 'But you're going to be, like it or not. I have things to say to you, young lady, that require just a tad more privacy than we've been allowed so far.'

She glared up at him, her arm still imprisoned in the gentle strength of his grip, only to find herself confronted by a grin of such total, boyish mischievousness that he might have been six years old again.

'I might come ten thousand miles to take you to lunch—or dinner, as it were—but I certainly wouldn't come that far for such a skinny little body,' he said in an intimate whisper, bending to whisper the message into her ear.

'You're impossible!' But she couldn't suppress a grin of her own.

'I am indeed,' he agreed, but his grip on her arm was more than just possible, and his impish grin displaced any suspicion that her response might have created for the few people who shared the lobby with them.

What if she screamed? Anne wondered. What if she stacked on a fair-dinkum blue, to use the Australian term for creating a scene of spectacular proportions?

But she wouldn't, of course, and they both knew it. More importantly, Steele knew it. He could have thrown her over his shoulder and carried her into the lift, and somehow he would have convinced everyone watching that it was perfectly acceptable behaviour and, more, that she was enjoying it!

As if feeling her relax, he eased his grip on her arm; now it would appear to any onlooker as merely tender, loving.

Anne shrugged off his hand entirely as the lift opened and stepped forward ahead of him, aware as she did so that it was only what he'd expected, what he'd intended all along. An elderly couple riding up with them glanced at each other and smiled, clearly entranced with this apparent display of affection. They must be blind, Anne thought, not to see that her own look held anger, resentment and distrust.

But of course they weren't reading her expression, she realised; they were seeing Steele Murdoch's lying attitude, the slightly amused but overtly gentle look he beamed down at her, creating a flush in her cheeks,

a perkiness to the tilt of her head. And with the lift
as crowded as it was she had no real choice but to
accept his arm around her shoulders, pulling her close
against him as if to protect her from the other oc-
cupants of the rising cubicle.

Carrying her sheepskin coat, she was none the less
far too warm, far too aware of the strong, muscular
warmth of the body pressed against her by his grip.
Steele Murdoch, she knew, appeared deceptively civilised. In his city suit, apart from the deep Australian
tan, he might have stepped out of any business office,
might have been a typical Canadian lawyer, stock-
broker, banking executive.

It made her think of an Australian television com-
mercial about a child in overalls being declared 'Foreman material', and she smothered a chuckle at the
memory. No foreman material in Steele Murdoch, she
thought—he was executive material or better, if de-
scribable by any such simple definition.

But there was less to chuckle about when they
emerged from the lift and she found herself alone with
an autocrat who marched her down a hallway and
kept a proprietorial grip on her arm as he let them
into what was more than just a simple hotel room.

Far more, she realised with a quite surprising burst
of insight. And would have laughed at herself, but
for the trouble of explaining why! What else to expect
of Steele Murdoch than to stay here in this hotel, in
a truly posh 'executive' room with its carefully contrived greenery and the large jacuzzi with its mirrors
and carpeted steps forming part of the room's décor,
not simply a part of the bathroom? The whole effect
was just so opulent, so typically overdone that she
would have loved to be able to laugh out loud.

'Make yourself comfortable,' he said briskly, tossing her coat over a chair. 'And stop looking as if you're afraid I'm going to ravish you, because I'm not.'

Anne bristled at the smoky humour in his eyes as he let go of her arm and stood back, eyes roaming over her body as if she were something he'd just purchased on a whim.

'Although actually,' he said, his voice dangerously soft, 'it wouldn't be that bad an idea if I had the time to feed you up a bit first. I'd have thought Canadian men would like their women with a bit of meat on them, considering this shocking climate they've got to live with.'

'You know the old saying,' Anne retorted. '"The nearer the bone, the sweeter——"'

'I might have a look at your mother while I'm here,' he interrupted as if she hadn't spoken, and her mouth snapped shut in astonishment. 'I know you've got a lot of her disposition; it'd be interesting to see what kind of figure you'll have when you grow up.'

'That...that's *gross*!' she cried, but Steele continued, a wry grin playing round his lips as if he were delighting in her discomfort.

'It's not surprising you don't write to the old fellow; you'd be pushing to find the energy, I'd reckon, the amount of weight you've lost. Maybe I'd best not offer you a drink after all, lest you get full as forty cats and try to ravish *me*.'

'Don't hold your breath,' Anne snapped, finally regaining her pluck. 'It would take more grog than you've got here to make me that desperate. And anyway...'

She paused then and shook her head in futile anger at the realisation that she'd once again been manipulated by Steele Murdoch, whose eyes were alight with unholy fires as he stepped forward and took her in his arms.

'Ah, Wombat, you're a worry,' he said in a peculiar voice as his lips descended to claim hers and his strong fingers played an electric tune down her spine.

His touch did more than create music that tingled throughout her body; it evoked memories she would rather didn't exist, much less dominate her reaction to his voice, his touch, his very presence.

Her lips ignored the plea from her brain, moulding themselves to his with a well-remembered ease. Her arms lifted as if under hypnosis to wrap themselves around his neck, pulling his mouth more tightly against her own. She tasted the warmth of his breath, revelled in the touch of his fingers as he caressed the small of her back, but all the while her mind was screaming a silent, *No*! which neither Steele nor her traitorous body seemed to care about.

As his fingers moved with devilish certainty across the swelling of her hips, Anne felt herself shifting within his grip, felt the throbbing of his arousal against her tummy, the equal throbbing of her nipples when one of his hands moved to touch her breast with a fiery impatience.

'No...*no*!' Now her objection was vocal, struggling past lips that tingled with his kiss, crying out for more even as her voice cried out for him to stop, for this madness to be halted before it passed all semblance of control. She was writhing in his arms, partly in a desperate bid to escape, but also in a wanton lust for more of his kisses, more of his caresses, more of *him*!

Her mouth trembling, eyes filling with tears of passion and sheer rage, she blinked furiously and found herself meeting eyes that fairly blazed with . . . laughter?

Thrusting her hands against his chest, Anne forced a modicum of distance between them, raising her eyes to see the curve of his lip, the disdainful start of a sneer that confirmed her judgement. He *was* laughing at her!

And then, thank heaven, he was also releasing her, stepping just one stride backwards to put that vital bit of space between them.

'Now that I've got your attention . . .' he drawled, and his sneer became, if anything, more obvious. Anne didn't give him a chance to finish; she lashed out without warning, her slashing, stabbing finger-nails narrowly missing one tanned cheek.

'Bastard!' she cried, reeling away to put even more space between them. 'Bastard . . . bastard . . . bastard.'

'You should have quit using that word by now,' he said with infuriating calm. 'It isn't so readily accepted a swear-word at this end of the world as in Australia, or so I've been given to understand.'

And as she glared up at him, speechless in the face of his calm reaction to her fury, yet crouched, cat-like, ready to scratch out his eyes if he gave her the slightest chance, Anne was amazed to see him reach out, palms upward in a placating gesture.

'Settle down,' he droned. 'I said I wouldn't ravish you, and I won't. I was only trying to get a bit of that sexual tension out of your system so we could talk like rational adults.'

'Humph!' It was all she managed to say, and even that single grunt of defiance seemed to her to quiver with an unbearable lack of control.

Steele only grinned at her, his teeth gleaming against the darkness of his tan, his eyes gleaming likewise with what could only be laughter at her inability to oppose him without making a total fool of herself.

Anne stepped back, reaching over to where her coat was. 'OK... you've got my attention,' she snarled. 'For just as long as it takes me to put this on and go—so you'd better make the best of it.'

To hell with him, she thought. To hell with him and his arrogant ways and his damnable ability to get her goat, to touch her and turn her on like some human light bulb. She no longer cared what he thought of her, what her father thought, what *anybody* thought. All she could think of now was escape, escape to sanity, to freedom from this man with his hateful ability to manage her emotions, her feelings, her body.

'I plan to make the most of it, but it will take a bit more time than that,' Steele replied—too calmly. 'So may I suggest you take it easy, sit down and I'll pour you a drink? Then we can discuss this like civilised adults.'

'Civilised adults don't go around groping other civilised adults,' Anne retorted snappily. 'Nor do they insist on playing games. So you can put your drink where it'll do you the most good and either tell me what you think is so damned important or shove it along with the drink. I'm not staying, and that's that!'

Steele shook his head, a gesture which only served to make her more angry. It was just as if he were dealing with a spoiled child; his entire attitude broadcast that message.

'I want to talk to you—seriously,' he said, 'about your father.'

'What's between me and my father is none of your rotten business,' she retorted, guilt giving her just the amount of courage she needed to defy this man who knew her too well, and knew all too well how to manipulate her.

'What's between you and your father is exactly nothing at all,' Steele growled in reply. 'Which is the whole problem.'

Again he shook his head, this time with his jaw clenched in obvious anger and frustration. 'Oh, to hell with both of you!' he suddenly cried. 'You're both so damned immature and stubborn and self-centred that I don't know why I bother with either one of you.'

And to Anne's surprise he whirled and slammed open the door to the room, turning then to glare at her through cold, hostile black eyes. 'Right! Go, if that's what you want. I can't imagine why I should have expected any other reaction; you and your old man both reckon running away is the only answer to just about every problem there is.'

They stood there then, glaring at each other and shying the occasional glance at the open door as if waiting for some newcomer to enter their private argument.

Anne wanted to go; she wanted in the worst way to just flee through that enticing open doorway and escape from this angry, handsome foreigner. But she couldn't. She stood there as if rooted to the floor, locked into the confrontation by Steele Murdoch's angry eyes, if nothing else.

If only, she thought . . . if only she'd never gone to Australia, never actually met her father, never met Steele Murdoch, never . . .

'Well?' The question emerged as a growl, so soft that she nearly didn't hear it.

'Well . . . what?'

'Are you staying or going?'

'What do you think?' she snapped.

'Why should I bother?'

'Because you started all this,' she cried. 'You're the one who came ten thousand miles to take me to *lunch*—or had you forgotten that?'

'To deliver your Christmas present, seeing I was going to be here in your city anyway,' he corrected her. 'Which doesn't answer my question. Why should I bother thinking about whether you stay or go? You'll do what you please in any event.'

'Too right I will!' she shouted, grabbing up her coat and striding to the beckoning doorway—then paused, knowing she'd already lost. Worse, knowing that *he* knew it too. She turned back, closing the door as she did so, then looked round the room with as much scorn as she could muster.

'I'm really rather surprised you didn't set yourself up in one of the *theme* rooms here,' she sneered. 'I'd have thought something like that would be right up your alley.'

Steele's reply was a look of utter scorn as he stalked across the room to rummage through his briefcase and then returned to brandish a colourful brochure in her face.

'And which, pray tell, would you have expected me to choose?' he asked. 'Would all this have been easier for you if I were staying in . . . a Roman room, with white marble statues, a round, velvet-covered bed with silk draperies and an authentic Roman bath? Or maybe the Hollywood room, with...a patented carpet with twinkling lights throughout? Or...' and he lapsed into a parody of a Southern accent '...y'all want me to sleep in a pickup truck?'

'I rather fancy the Arabian room of A Thousand and One Nights,' she replied after a careful study of the brochure. 'Or maybe the Polynesian room—provided you could manage the choice between the custom waterbed or the erupting volcano. Difficult choice.'

'Having you around is equivalent to any number of erupting volcanoes, but I'll keep the rest in mind. Now are you going to come and sit down and have a nightcap, or just stand there heaping abuse on me from a great height?'

'Only if you promise to get on with it and tell me *why* I'm here,' Anne told him. 'You didn't come all this way just to tell me that my father and I are both immature and stubborn and self-centred, true as it may be. Not that it's any of your business! *And* it's insulting.'

'Only because it's true,' he shrugged, turning away to collect two glasses and start filling them from a bottle whose very appearance brought back memories that startled Anne.

'Piper's Brook,' she cried excitedly before she realised what she was doing—then sobered instantly and declared, almost disdainfully, 'Trust you not to be going without what you consider the necessities of life. I suppose you ignored all the customs laws and smuggled in half your suitcase full of the stuff.'

'Hardly a necessity, but certainly one of life's small treasures,' he smiled, setting down the bottle. The wine, produced in northern Tasmania in small but growing quantities and usually sold almost before it was bottled, had a superb and justified reputation.

'And it is almost Christmas, after all,' Steele continued, 'surely a reasonable occasion to dip into a drop of this 1989 Rhine Riesling?'

He handed her the glass with a mock-bow of equally fake servility, then lifted his own glass in a toast.

'To... Christmas,' he said, then added something under his breath that Anne didn't quite hear—and if she had didn't quite understand.

'I was,' he revealed when she broached him on it, 'merely adding a small personal wish that you'd be seeing your father again soon.'

'Why?' The small sip of the excellent wine suddenly tasted sour in her mouth. Suspicion-soured; Steele Murdoch hadn't covered up fast enough, or well enough.

Now, however, he tried. 'It seemed like a good wish for a Christmas when you're apart,' he said. 'I drank a similar toast last year, with both him and your stepmother. Didn't work then either.'

'You're not telling me something,' Anne accused.

'I don't want to tell you,' he agreed, 'although in part it's why I'm here, or you're *here*, if you prefer.'

'I'm not going to like it either. I can tell,' she mused aloud, only to recoil with a start as she looked up to see the bleak, angry, icy look in his eyes.

'I certainly hope not,' he said in a voice that was even colder than his eyes, cold as the prairie winter outside. 'But it isn't your liking it or otherwise that I'm concerned with.'

'Well, stop beating around the bush and tell me, then,' she cried. 'It sounds as if it'll give you intense pleasure. Well, come on, let's have it. Has Monique left him and he's about to fly over here to cry on my shoulder, or has he finally cracked the world book market and wants me to come back and help him spend the money?'

'You,' Steele snarled with a look that was as hot as it was icy, 'are a self-centred little bitch who wants her bottom kicked. You and your father deserve each other; it's a shame to spoil two houses with you!'

Then the fierceness ran out of his eyes in a flood of such sadness that Anne could hardly credit it. And he sighed, then said quietly, sincerely, 'He's maybe dying, Anne, and I know he'd like—*love*—to see you again before he does ... *if* he does!'

CHAPTER FOUR

DYING! The word struck at Anne like a hammer blow, not one bit softened by Steele's gentle voice. She felt the glass slipping from her fingers, barely noticed him reach out to catch it before it fell. The blood rushed from her head and she felt her knees turn to water, saw the room swaying, the very pictures on the wall suddenly tipping sideways.

Then strong hands gripped her. She was lifted, carried, held as he moved over to deposit her on a sofa like some enormous, boneless parcel.

Then he was moving away, a blur in her suddenly tear-filled eyes, returning a moment later to press her glass into her hand, carefully curling her fingers round the stem. His fingers moved to touch her cheek, brushing aside the hair, resting on her temple.

'I'm sorry,' he said. 'I...didn't really mean to dump that on you so harshly.'

Any way would have been harsh, Anne found herself thinking, not that it mattered very much.

'How...why...what's the matter with him?' she finally managed to ask, the room still blurred, his face equally so, but at least everything now was still; she didn't feel any more as if she were swimming upside-down under water.

'*He* thinks cancer, or at least that's what I think he thinks. With your father it's impossible to guess. The man smokes like a chimney, so it wouldn't surprise me. Lungs, prostate—who knows? I suppose *he* does, maybe!'

'Do you know all this, or are you just speculating?' Anne asked, and felt stupid having done so. Steele Murdoch wasn't a man to speculate about such things. He knew.

'A little of both,' he admitted with surprising candour. 'It doesn't take an Einstein to see he isn't well and hasn't been for some time. In fact,' he continued, 'I can say with typically wondrous hindsight that you would have seen it even while you were there, if you'd been looking. Not that you were, of course; you were too busy worrying about yourself, at that point.'

Anne gasped in surprise at how callous the remark sounded, then closed her gaping mouth at the realisation that he was totally, utterly right. But still . . .

'Which means *you* ought to have noticed too. I suppose you realise that?' she charged. 'Or had you just conveniently forgotten that?'

'I had not. If you weren't so feisty I'd have had a chance to say so, too,' he retaliated. And then, surprisingly, he softened his entire attitude.

'I just realised how that must have sounded to you,' he admitted. 'And it wasn't quite what I'd intended to say. Of course I should have noticed, and in fact I *did* notice, but . . . well . . . my mind was sort of on other things most of the time then.'

Anne glared at him, suspicious now. He was . . . not really lying, but hiding something. She was sure of it. And all logic said it was something to do with him and Monique. She'd bet on it.

'And what about Moni . . . my stepmother? Did she just conveniently not notice either? Or did she have her mind sort of on other things most of the time too?'

Which was a catty, childish, totally unfair accusation. And both of them knew it. Anne shrank from Steele's scornful glare, seeing in his frosty black eyes a picture of herself that she didn't like at all.

'You've got some kind of a hate on for her, haven't you? She's his wife and I dare say she loves him, but she's not his keeper either. Much less,' he added with another frigid scowl, 'is she the type to be ignoring his health and letting him run himself to the grave sooner. *And* you know it, which makes your shirty little digs all the more...'

Surprising? Anne didn't—couldn't—be sure just how Steele had intended to finish his remark. She was astonished with herself for having said such a thing, because she *did* know that Monique loved her father, or at least cared for him. The fact that she also cared for Steele Murdoch was something else again, and deep in her heart Anne knew *that* was what coloured her feelings for a woman who'd never done her one iota of harm.

'You're right,' she admitted after a long, sobering pause of introspection. 'It was a very childish thing to say, and I'm sorry.' She didn't add that she was still more than half convinced there was much more between her stepmother and Steele Murdoch than appeared on the surface.

He only shrugged. 'She isn't going to know, so it hardly matters.'

But it did matter. It mattered because saying it had only dropped Anne even further in Steele's estimation. If that was possible. And it didn't help her own self-esteem either. She *wasn't* the kind of person she was sounding like! Wasn't—and never had been. Except, it seemed, when Steele Murdoch was around to stir her emotions and twist up her mind.

He'd done it right away from the very first meeting, an incident that paled by comparison—in terms of Steele's effect on her—with some of their clashes since.

Tonight, she realised, might be no exception.

'What are you asking of me?' she said, now having to force the conversation because he too had drifted off into thoughts he obviously wasn't going to share with her. 'I mean, do you expect me to find some way of going to Australia for another visit? Soon? Or is he planning to come here and you're afraid I'll spoil it for him if he does?'

'I don't know.'

'What do you mean, you don't know? You must know! Or did you just bring along the news as a bit of gossip to throw in if you happened to meet me on the street?'

The words flew out before she really thought, and Anne winced, but too late. Now, she thought, she was dumping on Steele because of her own injured feelings, and, while he might certainly deserve it from before, he didn't now.

'I'm sorry,' she pleaded quickly. 'That was un-called-for.'

'Seems to be the story of your life,' he grunted. He didn't seem all that hurt or even vaguely concerned by her slander. 'But going back to your question—yes, I think there is a chance he'll have a go at coming back. He's mentioned it, although how serious he was I wouldn't dare guess. And whether you have anything to do with that possibility I also wouldn't dare guess. He did say something about seeing your mother as well. Said it might be time to "lay a few ghosts", but only he knows if he was speaking literally or figuratively. Or even if he was remotely serious about it in the first place; he was fairly well in his cups, as I recall.'

'Mum would have kittens!'

'Hardly a new experience for her,' Steele murmured unkindly, then softened the rather caustic remark by adding, 'And if he took Monique along to the meeting I expect the kittens wouldn't be the half of it.'

'If he took Monique along, there'd be blood on the floor before it was over,' Anne mused.

Steele looked at her, curiously, she thought, then looked away, got up and refilled his glass. Anne's was still hardly touched.

'And what about your sister? How do you reckon she'd react to a visit from the old man?'

Anne shrugged. She and her sister were far from close. They'd fought like cat and dog throughout their growing-up years and, while they stayed in touch, some of the hostility remained.

'Only she knows,' she said. 'After all, *she* hasn't even seen him since she was seven, and now she's married, with kids of her own. I doubt if she'd recognise him on the street.'

'I'm not that sure *you* would. But that's hardly what I meant.'

'I *know* what you meant! And I said I don't know. It isn't something we talk about all the time, you know?'

'Are you trying to tell me you didn't talk about it before you came to Australia the first time, much less after you got back? Come now, Anne.'

'That was a long time ago,' Anne blustered. 'I think I've only seen her once since I got back, and that was at Mum's. Hardly the place for any great exchange of feelings on *that* subject.'

'Would she want to see him or not?'

Typical of Steele Murdoch, Anne thought. Cut through any excuses, ignore anything he didn't think relevant. Get right to the point.'

'I expect she would want to see him, if only to satisfy her own curiosity.'

'Hmm.'

Anne could have throttled him. This wasn't the first time she'd been faced with Steele Murdoch the enigmatic, a phenomenon she could easily come to dislike intensely. Breaking through that barrier, until he was quite ready to say whatever was on his mind, had proved in the past to be nothing short of impossible. She might as well talk to the wall.

'Hmm—what?' she tried, expecting nothing.

'Just hmm,' he replied, not being evasive, just his usual stubborn self, she thought. Then she had a sudden, horrific idea!

'He's already on his way,' she challenged. 'Or else he's already here, and you're just trying to soften me up, to get me ready for some awful reconciliation scene.'

'If that were the case, he could have brought your Christmas present himself,' Steele pointed out. Nice, that. Suitably evasive without forcing him into a direct lie. Anne wasn't fooled.

'He *is* here, isn't he?' she demanded. 'Or at least on the way? The present part of it means nothing; I've seen you lot plotting and scheming before, remember?'

He might not, though she doubted it. But she certainly remembered that Christmas in Tasmania. She would never forget the deviousness and ingenuity the two men had utilised to ensure that both she and Monique had no idea what they were getting for Christmas, no idea at all—despite the fact that the presents were right there in front of their noses virtually the entire time. And they'd been warned about it all, what was more!

'I can remember when I was a lad,' her father had said over dinner one evening when Steele was there—and when hadn't he been? Anne wondered now—'and my mother—your grandmother—gave both my father and me identical red shirts for Christmas. Shirts that she made herself, on her sewing machine. And she did it right there in front of both of us, although not at the same time. Blatant deception, sleight-of-hand, almost. Whichever of us was there could *see* her making the damned things; we were living in the country at the time, in a two-car garage, so you could hardly miss her. And all she did was tell each of us she was making the shirt for the other. Now I was pretty young, so maybe I can be excused for not noticing, but I never did figure out why my father didn't notice. You'd reckon, after all, that a grown man could look at a shirt being sewn and tell the difference between his size and mine. But he didn't, or at least he never let on, and I prefer to believe he was as fooled by it all as I was.'

The tale, further embellished, had drawn howls of laughter from Steele and Monique, but Anne hadn't really seen the humour of it until later, when she realised Steele had done almost exactly the same thing to her!

Right through the two months to Christmas he'd allowed her, even encouraged her, to watch him as he painstakingly carved the most delightful figurine out of a chunk of bird's-eye Huon pine, the rarest of Tasmania's unique timber species. And all the while that she watched the wood give up its secrets to his patient, magic fingers, she thought he was making a Christmas gift for Monique. Until Christmas morning, of course, when it turned up in her own stocking.

And her father, the crafty old devil, had yielded to expressions of interest by both her and Monique, buying each of them telescopically collapsible fly-fishing rods, then conning them individually into wrapping each other's—or their own—presents for him. And got away with it!

It had been, from many points of view, a truly memorable Christmas. The weather was all upside-down from Anne's perspective, of course, since Christmas in Australia was a summer affair. And at first she'd been certain it would suffer for that. Being in the middle of the major school holidays meant it was a time for extensive family travels; for many families it was celebrated not at home, but in a caravan on some beach or in a motel or even a tent.

For her, it had definitely lacked the feeling of being warmly and snugly shut in against the fierceness of winter weather, snow and blizzard winds. Instead, it had been a sweltering thirty-nine degrees, and the weatherboard farmhouse had had every door and window open in a vain attempt to beat the heat.

They'd eaten Christmas dinner at noon because of the heat, and even then it was a struggle to consume vast quantities of roast turkey, hot mince tarts, and

all the heavy foods of a traditional North American
or European Christmas. She had suspected, rightly,
that the food was all in her honour, and, after sam-
pling what Steele termed an Australian modern traditional Christmas dinner on New Year's Day, she had
found the cold meats, prawns and oysters, and salad
by the bucketful, a far more logical alternative in the
heat.

Even the tree had been different; her father had
insisted on them going up on a ridge behind the house
to chop down a small native cherry tree, which bore
only a superficial resemblance to what Anne considered a proper Christmas tree. Even decorated for
the occasion, it had looked and felt—to her—like an
impostor. Just like herself.

Steele was answering her question.

'He's not here, nor do I expect him to be here. And,
as for scheming, I suspect the only scheming your
father might be doing is how to keep Monique from
knowing how sick he really is.'

'That doesn't sound...right...' Anne ventured.

'Of course it isn't right. It's anything *but* right—
but it's your father. He just sits up there on his
mountain, his body going all to hell and his writing
not much better, fighting his own personal devils
alone. One of which,' he said with a shake of his head,
'is his word processor, that infernal machine that's
got a bit of the cat in its breeding, I swear.'

'Now you're making no sense at all,' Anne said,
concerned at how true his general remarks were, with
hindsight, but totally confused by the last comment.

'People think they own cats, but in reality it's the
other way round,' Steele replied. 'Your father's that

way with his machine; every time he turns it on, the damned thing takes control.'

Partially mollified, even seeing a modicum of truth in what he'd said, Anne sought more. 'And you're implying that I'm one of his "personal devils" as well?' she asked, expecting him to say yes, the worst.

'Not really,' was the surprising reply. 'Although now that he's old enough to have a sense of his own mortality, I suspect you and your sister are part of the ongoing problem of him and your mother.'

'And the unlaid ghosts.'

'Figuratively speaking,' he said, and his eyes took on a peculiar glow as they roamed undisciplined over her body, touching her breasts like a physical caress, stroking her legs. 'Maybe not only ghosts.' And now his grin was mischievous, the innuendo too obvious, as he intended. 'But the fact of the matter is simply that he's his own worst enemy. We all are, of course, but he takes it to extremes.'

Don't you play word games with me, Anne thought. And keep your lustful, smoky eyes to yourself too.

This while she felt her nipples throb and stiffen under his gaze, felt an undeniable softening warmth in her loins. *Figuratively* speaking indeed! Well, she was no ghost.

'All right. If he isn't here and he isn't coming, or at least you don't know that he *is*, would you mind telling me just what it is that you expect of me?' she asked, speaking slowly, deliberately, as if by this ploy she could extract some real intent from this convoluted discussion.

Steele looked at her silently, his eyes sharp, probing, but indecipherable. Well named, he was, and his eyes did all his advertising for him. They too were like steel, black steel.

'When do you finish up with the ankle-biters for the holidays?' he asked. Sudden, direct. Not unexpected, except for that.

'Another week, for most,' she replied. 'But there are children who'll have to be catered for right to the last minute, right up into Christmas Eve, most likely. And even during Christmas week there are a couple of situations where both parents will be working and I just couldn't——'

She was burbling, certain she knew what he was going to suggest, more certain that she couldn't—wouldn't—accept, wouldn't even seriously consider it, when he interrupted.

'Wait . . . until you're asked.'

Anne froze, her mind going into a deep-freeze of memory thought long dead. Back in time almost eighteen months. To when he had last said those exact words in that exact voice and destroyed her already fragile self-image, smashed it into a million pieces and scattered them like wallaby droppings outside the door of his cabin . . .

The day before she'd left to return to Canada, the day she'd tried her level best to seduce him, only to be rebuffed, to be told—very gently, to be sure, but bluntly—that she was too young!

All through her visit, Steele had set himself up as guide, companion, even confidant, but his romantic involvement had been kept under strict control. Oh, he'd kissed her, sometimes with a passion undeniable to them both. He'd undressed her, but only with his eyes, though her bikini left little to the imagination anyway. But every time things threatened to get out of hand, usually because she was totally infatuated and didn't bother to conceal it, he would balk, finding some way to extricate them both from what Anne was positive would be certain rapture.

Now, at this last of all possible opportunities, he'd done it again, and she was desperate, certain that if she could just manage to break down his reserves, make him see her as a woman in every possible, wonderful way, everything would click into place and all her dreams and fantasies would be realised, complete.

But he wouldn't, not even when she'd thrown herself at him, practically *begged* him to take her.

'Please, Anne,' he'd said. 'Please try and understand. I know this is what you want, what we both want, but the timing is just too...wrong. I wouldn't feel right about it, and neither would you, once you'd had time away from here, time to think about it. You've got enough on your plate trying to sort out your relationship with your father, never mind tossing in the kind of emotional dynamite you and I together would create.'

'But...but I *love* you!' she'd cried, playing her trump card, her last and only card.

'And I love you, which is why I'm trying my damnedest to keep from throwing you on to that bed and ravishing you until you miss the plane tomorrow,' he said grimly. 'Somebody in this crew has to show some will-power, and I guess it has to be me. Because now is simply not the time. Go back to Canada, see how things are there, see how you feel, give it some time.' And then, with one of his rare, blinding smiles, 'There's plenty of time. I may be a touch long in the tooth, but you...'

'I'm twenty-three,' she'd cried. 'And I'm not even a virgin, if that's what's bothering you.'

'You're about sixteen inside,' he'd told her, gently but implacably. 'And virginity, just for your information, is a state of mind. Whatever you've done in the past has nothing to do with it.'

The final, ultimate insult. Her sexual history, limited and juvenile as it had been, was irrelevant; she was just . . . too . . . young!

The words had turned love to hate in the twinkling of an eye, had turned a body languid with desire into one rigid with anger, seething with outrage.

His good intentions were rubbish, she'd screamed, flinging herself away from him, rushing to the door, wasting vital seconds trying to make it open the wrong way because she couldn't see through her tears, couldn't remember which way it opened, didn't care.

Once out, she had slammed the door so hard it should have shattered, just like her dreams, her needs, but not before she had screamed out her final vindictive outrage, calling on him to perform a physical impossibility, among other things. About the only thing she hadn't done, before fleeing the scene in a state of total defeat, was accuse him of the affair she knew he must be having with her father's wife.

And why she hadn't done that Anne still didn't know. Looking back now, she could only cringe at the memory of her humiliation. How gauche! How totally juvenile and self-centred and egotistical she'd been. With hindsight, and two years of supposedly growing up, she could see now how *he* must have seen her, how he must have laughed after she'd fled down the mountain, running the old logging tracks with her eyes blinded by tears, her mind blinded by pain and hurt.

He'd added insult to injury the next day by showing up to see her off at the airport, by calmly, smilingly, wishing her farewell, even kissing her goodbye. The devil! He'd known she couldn't scream at him, stab him with her nail file, whatever—known she simply wouldn't create any kind of scene in public.

So when he'd kissed her goodbye he'd done so in a manner that, to any onlooker, would have looked tender, loving. And she had been forced to respond in kind, though she'd spat, 'Pig!' at him through her rigid lips as she did so. He'd only kissed a little harder, forcing her lips open, forcing a response she didn't want to feel any more. Manipulative devil! He'd been right, of course. Not that she'd give him the satisfaction of admitting it. And she wouldn't. He was right too often—was probably right even now, but she wouldn't admit that either, not without a fight.

'It's not a matter of being asked,' she replied, snapping out of her reverie with a vengeance. 'Do you think I'm stupid or something, that I couldn't figure out what you're leading up to? Damn it, Steele, I'm not a child!'

Which gained her a sceptically raised eyebrow, the message of which was all too clear. Steele rose, shrugged off his jacket, returned to sit facing her.

'I expect you're presuming I'm going to ask you to fly back for another visit,' he said, 'when you haven't got the time and most likely wouldn't think of taking it if you could. And——' with a dubious smile '—I expect you're presuming I'd even offer to pay the shot.'

'Considering that I couldn't afford a trip to Calgary, which is only two hundred miles away, you can be sure I couldn't afford to just hop on a plane and flit off to Australia, anyway,' she told him.

'Do you even care if he dies?'

'Of *course* I care! How insensitive do you think I am?'

'That,' he said, 'is what I'm trying to find out.'

'Why? Why is it any of your business in the first place? He's my father, after all. Surely whatever's between us is just that—between *us*!'

'Frankly, I don't think you've got the faintest idea what's between you,' he said. 'You're both so damned self-centred sometimes. And—what's really the problem—so damned much alike!'

Anne felt the ice in that last remark, but she couldn't ignore the genuine feeling there. Steele Murdoch and her father were friends; Steele did care. About her father, anyway.

'Well, if it's so damned important, why isn't *he* doing something about it?' she demanded. 'You keep on at me as if it's all my fault, as if I'm the one who's responsible for the fact we don't get on, as if I'm the one who's supposed to change it all. What's the matter with *him*? Do you expect me to do it all? If he and I are so damned much alike, as you keep insisting, then surely...'

'You're younger and therefore supposedly more flexible,' was the bland reply. Simple, innocuous; but it had contained *that* word! Anne's mind shut out all logic, all reasonableness, just at the sound of it.

'You...you know-it-all!' she cried. 'How dare you put that load of rubbish on me? I tried for *six months*—the whole time I was there. Every day I tried!

And what did *he* do? Well, I'll tell you what he did—
he hid behind that massive great wall he's built around
himself. Oh, he came out occasionally and gave me
a pat on the head; sometimes he even devoted a few
minutes to try and talk to me, little fatherly chats. But
he never—*never*—came far enough out of himself so
I could even start to figure out who he is!'

'And you did?'

'Well, of cour...' And she halted. Because she
hadn't; she hadn't come any further out from behind
her personal fortress than her father had. And they
both knew it; so did Steele.

'I tried,' she declared. 'You can't argue about that.'

'And you think he didn't?'

'I...no, I suppose I don't really think that. Looking
at it from...now, I realise that he just didn't know
how. And yes, before you say it, I didn't make it any
easier for him.'

'I doubt if he expected you to.' And Steele's smile
now was suddenly as she remembered—warm,
genuine. 'And I'm pleased to see this couple of years
has given you a better perspective on the whole thing.
I wish I could say the same about Curtis, but it
wouldn't be true, which is sad. He thought he had to
be a father, and that's what he tried to be, believe it
or not. Certainly it was a mistake.'

'A mistake? He mightn't have done a very good
job of it, but how can you say it was a mistake?' Anne
challenged, only after the words were out realising she
had leapt to her father's defence.

'No experience,' he shrugged. 'I might as well have
tried to pilot the plane that brought you here. Wanting
to do something and being able to are often
quite different.'

'I didn't have any experience either,' Anne said. No sudden perceptiveness, this; just the utterance of something she'd felt for more than two years but never been able to admit, much less out loud.

Steele didn't, for a change, say anything. He just sat there and looked at her with the most curious expression in those smoky, fathomless eyes—eyes that seemed able to penetrate all her defences, to see right through her to where the real Anne Dunne lived. It was disconcerting, almost spooky.

'I haven't written to him since just after last Christmas,' she found herself admitting. The statement was flat, emotionless.

Steele nodded but said nothing.

'I . . . I didn't know what to say. I never know what to say. He writes to me as if . . . as if I were some sort of distant relative, not . . . not as if I was his *daughter*.' She paused then, peering into his eyes, seeking . . . something. Reassurance, encouragement?

'It isn't that his letters aren't—well, friendly or whatever. They're always pleasant and informative; he always tells me what's going on, especially if it involves something from when I was there, something I know about. He usually mentions . . . you.'

No lie, that. Not that she'd admit how avidly she searched her father's letters for just those mentions.

'But they just aren't the kind of letters that really demand immediate replies,' she continued, not daring to slow long enough to question why, all of a sudden, she should be telling Steele Murdoch all this. 'So I don't answer them immediately, and then . . . then I just don't get around to answering them at all.'

A shrug. Of understanding? Or just polite uninterest? At least he seemed to be paying attention.

'It's understandable. If you asked him, I suspect he feels much the same, in many ways. I know I've heard him comment that it was damned difficult trying to be a father for that time when he didn't know what he was doing and had no idea if he was on the right track or the wrong one.'

Then he added the bombshell, the question Anne had been half expecting, totally dreading.

'Is that the same kind of reasoning you used in not answering *my* letters?'

'No,' she said calmly, prepared for this even though fearing it. 'No, it wasn't.' And she determined to clarify her feeling no further, no matter what the provocation.

'Umm...' And he left it there. Changed the subject completely and, as usual, without warning. 'Would you consider phoning him?'

Anne looked at him, astonished. 'Now?'

'Why not? It's...about five...six o'clock in the evening there now; he ought to be in fit shape to talk to you.'

But am I in fit shape to talk to him? she found herself wondering. Much less with Steele sitting here listening to every word, analysing everything I say, everything I don't say. It would be impossible.

'No.' She put firmness into her voice. 'No...not now, if you don't mind.'

'I could always slip down to the bar for a drink, if it's the privacy factor.'

Perceptive devil! 'It's not entirely that,' she said, and wondered why she should have to justify the decision. 'It's that I'm—well, just not prepared. It's not something I'd do just off the top of my head, for goodness' sake.'

Again that shrug that indicated acceptance, indifference or too, too much understanding.

'You have to *prepare* yourself? Communications in your family must be something to behold,' he said quietly. 'I get these amazing mental pictures of people sitting around doing these strange confidence-building exercises before they pick up a telephone. Making lists of what to say, what not to say, what tone of voice to use. I'm not surprised you and your sister aren't close.'

'But...but...' Anne found it impossible to make him understand. 'But what do I say? I can't just pick up a phone and...and...'

His laugh was genuine enough, but the humour in it was as black as his eyes.

'You say, "Hello, Father. This is your darling younger daughter phoning to wish you Merry Christmas." And he'll say, "Murdoch's put you up to this, and don't bother to deny it." And you'll say, "Too right he did. And just as well too. Is it true you're trying to drink yourself to death, because if you are I'd like the chance to put *my* opinion on that subject, which is..."' And Steele paused, fixing Anne with his eyes. 'Over to you,' he said with a nod. 'I'll arrange for the call, if you like. But, judging from the look on your face, I think you'd best have another drink first.'

'Are you sure you don't want to choreograph the rest of the conversation before I do?' she quipped. 'That way you can be sure not to miss anything while you're out of the room while I make it!'

'No, I don't think so,' he replied, rising to refill her glass, his little victory complete and so, so obvious. He put the bottle down, handy to the phone, she noticed, then picked up the receiver and spoke briefly into it, reciting from memory the number she would have had to look up.

'They'll ring when they get through to Hobart,' he said then, flashing her an enigmatic grin as he picked up his jacket and walked to the door. He was closing it behind him when he leaned back into the room and threw her one of those brilliant, heart-melting smiles.

'Don't forget your lines, eh?' And he was gone, just as the phone shrilled her to panic stations.

Anne didn't believe what she was hearing at first. Then she found herself screaming across ten thousand miles, 'That damned Steele Murdoch set this up! You're saying just what he said you'd say!'

'Well, he would, wouldn't he?' Curtis Dunne answered, and she could detect no obvious evidence from his voice that he was sick. 'I'd have told you a long time ago he's a devious, manipulative devil—if you'd asked me and if I thought you'd believe me.'

'I wish you had,' Anne retorted hotly. 'But what I want to know is if he's telling the truth. Is he?'

'Of course not. Oh, I drink a bit, probably a bit too much, but he's making mountains out of molehills.'

'And I suppose you're not sick either?' she demanded, a deep, empty feeling in the pit of her stomach at that...something in his voice that shouted to her that he was lying.

'Did he tell you that?' Again that forced indignation, that infinitesimal nuance that proclaimed the lie. He's as transparent as glass, she told herself. Not fooling me, or anybody else. Probably not even trying. She was astonished, then angry.

'Let me speak to Monique, please,' she demanded, brooking no arguments, no excuses. She would get to the bottom of this now, right now!

He didn't even bother to try and put her off. Her command brought first a long silence, then her step-mother's lilting accent.

'Merry Christmas, *chérie*.'

'Merry Christmas to you too,' Anne said. 'Or I hope so, anyway.' And then she jumped in with both feet. 'Is what Steele Murdoch's been telling me true? Is . . . Dad . . . has he got cancer or something, some-thing that's . . . killing him?'

The reply was in that same lilting voice, but now the voice held something Anne realised she had seldom noticed before, but which must have been there, be-cause she recognised it immediately. Behind the velvet voice was a black despair, an acceptance of an un-wanted but unavoidable reality. And an iron will, a fierce determination to fight, even knowing it was a losing battle from the start. And a strong sense of caring that Anne realised she hadn't expected.

'He is sick. He says he is not. It is not for me to say; if he does not accept it, then maybe he is not. Who can say? Only a doctor, maybe.'

'Which means, I take it, that he is sick and won't damned well admit it?' said Anne. 'And that he won't even *see* a doctor? What do *you* think—lung cancer? Prostate? Bowel cancer?'

'I cannot say; he does not listen to me anyway. Maybe he listens to you,' was the evasive reply, fol-lowed by a short silence until her father came back on the phone.

'Did he at least give you your Christmas present before he started unloading this great heap of rubbish?' he demanded.

'Yes,' she replied, her voice a whisper as reality sped through the telephone. 'And it isn't rubbish, is it? You *are* sick.'

'Just a bit under the weather these last few months,' he replied evasively. 'The heat, I expect. I'm happiest here in the winters.'

'Why do you lie to me?' she sighed. 'I'm your daughter, damn it. I love you. I care what happens to you.'

Which created a long and expensive silence while both of them, Anne presumed, thought about what she'd just said. What had come out of her mouth without preparation, without even conscious thought. The truth. She did love him, and she did care.

'I . . . I'm pleased, because I love you too,' was the equally astonishing reply—Curtis Dunne's single and isolated foray into the world of her feelings and his own. 'But don't worry; I'll be all right. Monique takes very good care of me, as you know,' he continued as if that deeply meaningful lapse hadn't even occurred, as if neither of them had just said out loud what they hadn't been able to say, face to face, during Anne's entire visit.

'I'll just put her on again; she has something else she wants to say,' her father went on. 'Merry Christmas to you, if I forgot to say it before, and please pass on my regards to your mother when you see her.'

It hardly even registered; nor did Monique's casually asking, 'Is Steele Murdoch all right? He was a bit—

well, *étrange* ... strange, when he left. Perhaps he is ... not well?'

'He's the same devious, cunning devil he's always been,' was Anne's almost angry reply. Her mind was no longer in this conversation; it was busy planning, scheming. Just as that damned Steele had intended!

Hanging up the telephone, she didn't even bother to finish her drink. She grabbed up her coat and handbag and fled the room, unwilling to face Steele just now, knowing she didn't want to relay the conversation, didn't even want to talk to him. Not now! All she wanted was to be alone, to rummage through this new bag of emotions she'd found in her attic, this new sense of ... of belonging, of sharing.

She would go home, be alone with her thoughts, have a chance to thrash things through without his intervention, without his involvement and his striking ability to confuse her.

She fidgeted in front of the lift, shifting her weight from foot to foot. She hoped and prayed he wouldn't be getting out when it stopped, that he wouldn't be waiting in the lobby, expecting her to do exactly what she was doing.

But he wasn't, which was about the only saving grace of the entire evening, she thought, tramping through the winter night to where her car squatted lonely in the half-deserted car park.

She drove home slowly, carefully, but with only half her mind on what she was doing. The rest was busy planning what to pack, and how she could psych herself up to face Steele Murdoch with the decision that she just *knew* he'd expected all along.

CHAPTER FIVE

'BUT I want to go *now*!'

She probably sounded like a spoiled brat, Anne realised. But it was true—she did want to go *now*, so why shouldn't she say so?

'There isn't a spare seat until January the ninth.'

She knew that; he'd told her that a dozen times, and from the look on his face Steele was just about ready to *tell* her that he'd told her that a dozen times. He was getting distinctly cranky, Anne could see, and she took a fierce satisfaction in that.

'But surely they'd have seats available for... for situations of compassion,' she insisted.

'These are not compassionate grounds,' he said, his voice still even, gentle, but holding an edge now. He was definitely getting cranky. Anne couldn't resist pushing. He deserved it, after all, for letting three days go by without calling her, without making any contact at all.

'But you said he was dying! Surely that's compassionate grounds.'

'He may outlive you, if you keep this up,' he said, his black eyes smouldering. 'Give it a rest, Anne. It's three days until Christmas, we've got you booked for the ninth, and I'm reasonably certain your old man will survive that long. There may not even be anything wrong with him at all, for that matter. Until we can convince him to see a doctor, nobody knows; we're all just speculating.'

'There had *better* be something the matter with him,' she said viciously, knowing she still had Steele on the hop. 'I've had to give up my job for this trip, you know. They wouldn't promise to hold it for me. I finish on Christmas Eve.'

'A small price for a return to a civilised country,' he replied around a mouthful of home fries. 'Although I will admit your mob doesn't do bad breakfasts. Not as good as the Americans', but quite passable.'

They were in a small café around the corner from the child-care centre, and Steele was steadily working his way through a gigantic breakfast of blueberry waffles, bacon, eggs, sausages and the home fries he professed to love. Anne was on her third cup of coffee, astounded that he could put away a meal that size at such an ungodly hour of the morning. Just the thought of it made her stomach go queasy, but she was no longer concerned about Steele's eating habits. It was his deviousness that bothered her more.

'Why do I have the suspicion you set this all up, somehow?' she probed. 'It's more than just coincidence, surely, that the only available seat just *happens* to be on the same plane you're going home on.'

Actually, she wasn't at all unhappy about the timing. It would give her time to sort things out with John, who hadn't even been told about her exodus yet—that was something which would require very careful handling, she knew—and maybe, just maybe, it would give her a chance to rustle up enough money to pay for the trip so that she wouldn't be dependent on Steele's generosity.

'We may need the time for your visa to come through. And wouldn't you rather have company? It's a helluva long journey—even stopping over in Hawaii to break it up a bit.'

'I didn't stop over at all when I went the first time,' she said. 'I think it was something like thirty-seven hours altogether, by the time I got to Hobart. Still, I won seventeen dollars playing gin rummy during the main part of the flight, which was an improvement on the bad movie they were showing. It was an Australian who taught me; I don't think he expected the lessons to be so expensive.'

'Some of us are fairly naïve where pretty girls are concerned,' said Steele ruefully. 'Does this mean I've got to learn the game some time in the next few weeks?'

'I can't imagine why,' Anne said, ignoring the compliment, refusing even to acknowledge it. 'I've never played it before or since. But it was nice to have pleasant company, yes.'

Even if it turned out that she was forced to accept his charity, she thought, it would only be a temporary thing. Whether she found the money before or after the trip, she would insist on paying back every single cent. And taking his charity didn't mean she had to accept him along with it; she'd make sure he had no illusions about that!

Steele had used the telephone to kick her out of a sound sleep that morning, calling nearly an hour before her alarm clock would have done so much more gently. 'I'll see you for breakfast,' he'd said with hardly a greeting, then named the place and hung up. Anne had no idea how he'd determined that the café did early breakfasts; *she* hadn't known, despite being in and out of there virtually every working day. He must have scouted the place thoroughly in advance, she thought. It would be just like him.

'I have to go to work in a few minutes,' she said, aiming to conclude the conversation and do exactly that. If she was going to be leaving immediately after the holidays, even without the job to come back to, there was much to be done about handing over to— of all people—Karen. A management decision in which Anne hadn't even been consulted, which made it all the more infuriating.

She must have growled her anger, because Steele looked over at her with one eyebrow raised in what might have been a questioning look. But he asked nothing.

'Pity you aren't going with a decent breakfast inside you,' he commented. 'I'm not surprised your temperament's gone to the pack, dealing with a massive great mob of screaming rug-rats on an empty stomach.'

'You're not my mother,' Anne snapped. 'And I wish you wouldn't sound like her.'

'We'll get you sorted out on the trip home,' he said, ignoring her slight. 'Be easy enough to make you eat your veggies when you're buckled down and can't go anywhere.'

She had a mental picture of him force-feeding her like a baby bird, while a stewardess hung over his shoulder, doting on his every command, and almost laughed.

'Am I going to meet your mother, by the way?'

'I most sincerely hope *not*!' She could just imagine the way her dear mother would react to Steele Murdoch, the simpering and play-acting and gushy little flirtations. It would be quite, quite sickening.

'And I have to go,' she hurriedly added to avoid any explanation.

'Right. How about I see you here for lunch?' he said. 'I see they've got dry garlic spare ribs on the menu, and if the breakfast was any example, those certainly deserve a try.'

'I don't take lunches,' she replied without thinking, only to have him cock his head and smile mysteriously. All right, she thought, so I just revealed that I lied to him the day he arrived. But I'm damned if I'll admit it. 'I mean I can't now,' she said. 'There's so much to do, and all. The management would have kittens if I did.'

He shrugged, shifting his broad shoulders in a gesture that displayed them to wondrous advantage. Dressed casually today and with a seeming disdain for the Canadian winter—he had only a sweater on over his shirt and hadn't bothered with his sheepskin coat— he stood out because of his deep tan and, she had to admit, because he just *did*.

'So what are they going to do—sack you?'

'They could refuse me a decent reference, which I'll need when I get back and have to start looking for another job,' Anne told him. 'There's still something of a recession on here, in case you hadn't noticed, and jobs are hard enough to come by even with good references.'

'Always more top jobs than top people,' responded the man who, according to her father, was making more money than most adults before he'd finished high school. He'd never been unemployed in his life, Anne knew, not like her own dear John, whose sensitivity and the problems created by a trifling police record made it impossible for him to keep a job long even on those rare occasions he was able to find one. Problems he wouldn't face, she thought, if he had the ego and determination and sheer bloody-mindedness of the man across the table from her.

'Well, you don't get to be a "top" person with poor references,' she replied hotly. 'It's fine for you, but I've got a reputation to uphold.' Then she shook her head at just how ridiculous that statement was. Steele Murdoch's reputation was such that half his business dealings were done with a handshake, if that. He'll really be cranky now, she thought, and waited for an explosion that simply didn't come.

'You're right, of course,' he said in that calm voice that could be just so infuriating. 'So let's just say that *I'll* be here for lunch, and if you can manage it, fine, and if you can't I'll just have to wait to hear from you.'

It was a dismissal, she realised. Leaving her with the choice of joining him for lunch, or at least making an appearance, or being forced to wait on his convenience should she want to talk to him. *Need* to talk to him, she corrected herself. She didn't necessarily want to, but she very much might need to.

The problem was mostly forgotten during the worst morning Anne had ever experienced at work. Karen, having already been told of her forthcoming promotion, seemed to have decided she was already the boss, and hopelessly, maddeningly officious with it. Anne, already running on her nerves because of Steele, found it insane; she could only imagine another two days of such goings-on, and she didn't like the prospect one bit. At noon she abandoned ship; even lunch with Steele would be an improvement. Or would have been, except that he didn't seem in the least surprised to see her. He gave the impression, indeed, of having quite expected her. Smug, arrogant...

'Have you been running around town all morning like that?' she demanded, neglecting greetings for the satisfaction of getting her licks in first for a change. Steele still didn't appear to be bothering with a coat, and it was well below zero outside. 'You've got a nerve, trying to mother *me* when you go around in the winter dressed like that,' she accused. 'Is this the new macho image or something?'

'It gets a touch cool occasionally,' he admitted without batting an eyelid. 'But infinitely preferable to roasting every time I walk into a building. You Canadians must be a sickly lot, the way you keep your houses and shops warm. I reckon central heating will be the death of you.'

'But you had a coat on the other day.'

'Ah, but that's because I was walking around outside all morning, getting my bearings and trying to find your workplace without asking anybody. Which,' he continued—smugly, she thought—'I only just managed to do.'

Menus arrived, and Steele waved his aside, asking for the dry garlic ribs with a side-order of fries. 'And bring the salad *with* the rest,' he made a point of insisting, before turning his attention to Anne.

'This business of trying to fill you up with rabbit food before you get to the proper tucker is difficult to get used to, at my age,' he said. 'But, considering you've had a couple of hundred years of so-called bilingualism and still couldn't get it right, I suppose some of your strange eating habits are to be expected.'

'That's because your French is abysmal,' said Anne, whose own command of Canada's second langauge was non-existent. 'I suppose you're on about our calling the main course an entrée, which is what *you* call the appetiser that *we* call an aperitif. End of lesson.'

'Good. If that's the way you explain things to your rug-rats, I can assure their parents you're well out of it. Interesting, however. I can hardly wait for you to tell me what a beeyeltee is.'

'BLT,' Anne laughed. 'Bacon, lettuce and tomato sandwich, or bacon, lettuce and tomawto to you. I'd have thought a world traveller like you would have figured that one out.'

'Oh, I had; I just wanted to see how convoluted your explanation would be,' he retorted.

'I ordered it because I haven't got all day to spend on an executive lunch,' she snapped back. 'And because I like them.'

She didn't like what she saw next. Didn't like it all, and worse—she couldn't do a thing about it. Too late even to hide her head as John sauntered through the door with fire in his eyes.

'Karen said you'd be here,' he said without giving Anne a chance to think, much less speak. 'What's all this about tossing in your job and going back to Australia?'

'I . . . just haven't had a chance to tell you, that's all,' Anne said, stumbling over the words and then recovering. 'Now come and meet Steele Murdoch, who's an old friend of my father's.'

John extended a hand cautiously, as if Steele might bite it off, giving the older man a petulant stare as he mumbled a sort of greeting. But his attention was for Anne.

'Well, jeez, you might have told me. I mean, it's pretty awful having to hear it from somebody else like that. I mean . . .'

Steele, mercifully, cut him off from further whingeing and complaining by asking if he'd had lunch yet, then summoning the waiter with another menu.

'Bring the boy whatever he wants,' he said, in those few words expressing his mastery of the situation and clearly defining his role as host. And he kept it up right through the meal, skilfully sounding John out, leading him to voice his opinions about the trip and anything else he wanted to whinge about. It wasn't that difficult to do, Anne noticed. John was clearly overawed by the tall Australian, but couldn't resist leaping to every bait that was offered and especially to being the centre of attention.

But, true to form, once the meal was over he made a patently feeble excuse to get himself away before the bill arrived, pausing only long enough to assure Anne that he would see her that evening, when they would 'sort out this trip thing'.

By this time she was exhausted. It had been the worst hour of her life, she thought. Anything else simply paled by comparison. And her feelings weren't improved by the fact that she knew Steele had done it all deliberately, first leading John to make a fool of himself and then helping!

'I hope you're proud of yourself,' she said scornfully as she picked up her coat and prepared to return to the fray with Karen, which now seemed infinitely preferable. Especially as she realised John hadn't even said thank you for the meal.

Steele didn't even have the decency to pretend innocence. He just looked at Anne, shook his head sadly, and mouthed the words, Know thine enemy.

He waited until she was nearly to the door, having forced herself to thank him for the meal on both her and John's behalf, to halt her with a word, then say, soberly, 'Enjoy your evening.'

He might as well have slapped her, she thought, barging into the day-care centre with fire in her eyes and every nerve spoiling for a fight. Karen, not totally a fool, avoided her like the plague all afternoon.

The evening improved nothing. John was waiting for Anne when she got back to what she now thought of as her dingy little flat—at the very least, she wouldn't be coming back from Australia to *here*!—and despite their enormous lunch seemed to be expecting her to produce dinner for them.

Which she did, grudgingly, only to spend her cooking time and the rest of the evening listening to a litany of complaints that did everything but come out and accuse her of sleeping with Steele. In John's mind, obviously, the whole situation had been deliberately created just to spite him, just to make his world a bit less manageable.

'I don't know what you think you'll accomplish by all this,' he said. 'Except to have a really neat holiday. I mean, after all, if your father's sick he should go to a doctor. And he's got a wife to look after him, so what can *you* do? And...well...it's going to make things sort of difficult for me, you know?'

And on and on and on...until she finally managed to ease him out by promising to reconsider the whole thing. Not quite a lie, because she would, but she wouldn't change her mind and she knew it.

Anne felt like death. She made herself some hot chocolate, stared angrily at the supper dishes with a sudden memory flash of both her father and Steele happily washing up after she or Monique had cooked dinner, and growled a curse on John's head. They could damned well stay there until the next night, she thought, when she might demand that he wash up both lots.

But by the time the hot chocolate had done its work her temper had cooled and her will with it. She couldn't go to bed and get up to face that sink, so she did the dishes and settled down to a troubled rest that became insanely troubled when the telephone shrilled at her.

'What *do* you think you're doing, Anne? I spoke to that nice girl at your office during lunch; you weren't there, of course, when I called. How can you even consider going to Australia again? And who is this Murdoch person?'

Karen again! What was she doing—going out and broadcasting on the streets? And why, Anne wondered, had Karen not said anything to her about it during the afternoon? She knew the answer; it was because her mother rang so often for so little reason that even Karen wouldn't think it important enough to mention.

'If you knew about all this at noon, Mother, why did you have to wait until now to phone me?'

'Well, I didn't believe it, of course. And then I had . . .' Whereupon Anne was treated to one of her mother's better performances. This one ran the full gamut of emotions in a voice designed for high drama. There was guilt, suffering, pleading, wheedling, firm demands, not-so-firm demands—the works!

Anne listened, sort of. She'd heard it all before *ad nauseam*, but somehow had never seen her mother's manipulative nature quite so clearly for what it was. Whenever she got a chance to slip a word in edgewise, she would try, but twenty minutes later she gave up even that as a waste of time. So she waited for the record to run down, then got it all out in one burst.

'Mother, my name is Anne, not Eve. I'm not responsible for the original sin and every one since. I'm going to Australia because I must. I'm not going just to cause you worry and problems, and I'm not going just to spite you.'

Ten minutes later still, 'John is very upset too, Mother. I'm sure he won't be waiting when I come back.' This should have had some effect; her mother hated John with a passion normally reserved for the tax collectors and politicians of the world. And herself? Anne wondered. And looked at the clock again.

Five minutes more and her mother wasn't into repeat mode yet. Which was worrying; she should have been starting to run down by now if she wasn't going to start at the beginning again. At the first pause, Anne took a deep breath herself and plunged in with her trump card, knowing that if she didn't stop this she could be still enduring it at breakfast time.

'Dad sends his regards, by the way. And said to wish you a Merry Christmas.'

That did it. Anne used the breathless pause to rush in with, 'I have to go now, Mum, or I'll never get up for work. Love you. Goodnight.'

When five minutes had passed without the phone ringing again, she sighed with relief. She did love her mother, she thought, but it was hard, sometimes, because increasingly she was finding she didn't *like* her much at all. She turned the phone off, which she wouldn't have dared do while there was a chance that her mother might ring back, flopped into her bed, and drifted into sleep by counting the ways she might destroy Karen.

The next day was no better. Karen was insufferable, John was more so, until Anne had to tell him to just stop phoning her at work and she'd see him later. She did, but spent much of the time between comparing him to Steele Murdoch—unfavourably. John just wasn't, she had to admit, in the same class. Beside Steele he just . . . faded away. No substance, no . . . anything. When he left her that evening it was just as he'd arrived, with a complaint—this time that he wouldn't see her on Christmas Eve because she would be going to her mother's and he wasn't welcome and wouldn't go. But he would see her, he insisted, on Christmas morning, because she must remember she was invited to *his* mother's for brunch.

As she did the dishes, alone, her good intentions of the previous evening quite forgotten, Anne thought about Christmas brunch, and knew she wasn't going to be there. She'd given John his Christmas present already, so her conscience was clear on that score. What she would do for the day she had no idea and didn't particularly care, but John wouldn't be a part of it. And by morning she realised that was no great loss at all.

She woke to the morning of Christmas Eve, the centre's last day of operation until the New Year, with none of the anticipation she felt she should have had. It was her final day on the job, she'd have Christmas and then a week without distraction to plan for her trip. But it all felt...flat, somehow. She had Christmas shopping still to do, presents to wrap, and a list of other 'musts' as long as her arm. But no time. She'd be at work until six, with precious little time to spare and the guarantee of some parent being late. They knew nobody would dare just shove their little darlings out to wait in the cold, and there was always some parent, invariably a single parent, who would take advantage. Last Christmas Eve she'd been stuck there with one very tired, very confused toddler until nearly eight o'clock, while the child's mother, with no husband to worry about, had been enjoying an office party!

'Well, today that's your problem, Karen,' she stressed after arriving to find—surprise, surprise—that her replacement was not only on time for once, but early. And that Karen somehow had shed some of her officiousness overnight; she didn't even argue at the prospect of staying late if required. It wasn't enough to make Anne like her any better, but there was at least a chance now that she could finish out her time without open warfare.

Anne didn't even bother to confront Karen with having spilled her plans before she had found time to prepare her mother for the situation. The girl wouldn't have understood, and if she had she would have taken immense pleasure from her act, Anne was sure.

For herself, there was the unexpected pleasure of being given her final cheque, a splendid letter of reference, and the real bonus—being able to walk away free at noon! She could hardly believe her luck, and spent the remaining few hours looking over her shoulder, expecting some catastrophe. But by five to twelve, when she and the others had exchanged token

gifts and it was all but over, Anne could feel herself
like a sprinter in the blocks, getting ready to run while
she had the chance.

Her desk was cleared and she was picking up the
small box of her personal effects when the phone rang,
and she automatically reached out to answer it.

'I'm just calling to remind you about tonight,' her
mother said. As if she hadn't reminded her half a
dozen times already, usually just to reinforce the
dictum that John must not be part of the traditional
family Christmas Eve dinner. Anne's being late last
year had caused a minor hurricane of recriminations.

'There isn't going to be a problem this year, Mother.
I'm all finished now, as a matter of fact. I've got a
bit of last-minute shopping to do, and I'll be there on
time. I promise.'

'Of course you will, Anne; I'm not suggesting you
wouldn't. I just thought it would be nice if you had
time—and I'm so glad you will, because it makes
everything so very much easier—if you'd pick up your
friend Mr Murdoch on your way? It would save him
a fortune in taxi...'

Anne didn't hear the rest, *couldn't* hear it past the
roaring in her ears, the sudden feeling that she was
going to faint, perhaps even die!

'...certainly sounds a very nice man, dear. Extremely well spoken, I thought. And that voice...'

'Mother?' Anne thought she'd spoken aloud, but
she must have only whispered. Her mother never even
noticed.

'...said you'd pick him up at seven. It's right on
your way, after all. But you'll have to call him and
confirm that, of course. You will do that, won't you,
Anne? And be sure to wear something really pretty;

it isn't often we have a guest. There'll only be the
three of us, unfortunately. Kathleen and her family
won't arrive until tomorrow morning now, because
of . . . well, something or other. I didn't really understand the problem; you know how she is, so vague
about things. Now I must go because I have just *so*
much to do. Dinner will be at seven-thirty, and you
will remember to call Mr Murdoch, won't you?'

She hung up before Anne could say anything, much
less offer the suggestion that her mother, having mir-
aculously managed to track down Steele Murdoch in
a city of half a million people, should have him to
Christmas Eve dinner *by herself*!

Anne put the phone down as if it might leap up
again and bite her, then grabbed up her coat and
snowboots, bundled the box of personal effects under
the other arm, and fled.

CHAPTER SIX

STEELE was already inside the car, his presence almost overwhelming in the small interior, before Anne realised she'd forgotten to call him, had just driven up to the hotel entrance knowing, somehow, that he'd be there. The surprise wasn't that *he* was there; it was that she'd managed to summon the courage to be there herself!

'I nearly didn't come,' she said, ignoring his casual greeting, unable to ignore the closeness of him, the scent of his aftershave, the way he so casually tossed his sheepskin coat into the back. 'You'll freeze to death in this car without your coat,' she added hurriedly. 'The heater barely keeps the windshield clear, let alone keep people warm.' Her own coat was fully closed over the flimsiness of her sleeveless, backless green dress.

She'd almost opted for a deliberately casual look; jeans and a sweater made more sense in this weather than a dress that couldn't keep a mouse warm. But she'd chickened out in the end, knowing her mother would make the evening unbearable enough without giving her additional ammunition.

'I'll survive. And why did you come if you didn't want to?' he asked with a grin that almost answered his own question. He knew perfectly well why she'd rather not face the evening, and knew equally well that she'd never have been able to do anything but what she had done.

'It was better than the alternative, which is having Mother bitch about it forever if I didn't,' she admitted. And then, with a sudden, terrifying insight, 'Did you set this up? I'll bet you *did*,' she accused, wondering how she could be so stupid. Of course he'd set it up; no way known to man could her mother have found him and arranged this evening all by herself.

'On the spirits of Christmas past, present and future, I swear I had nothing at all to do with it,' he swore, hand over his heart. 'Apart from accepting, of course, and you could hardly expect me not to.'

'The hell I couldn't,' she retorted. 'No, I take that back. If my mother decided you ought to be there, even *you* couldn't get out of it. Not that I'd expect you even to try.'

'I thought it was a most generous invitation,' he replied, not bothering to hide his grin. 'Stranger in town and all that, certain to be feeling lonely and bereft in a foreign country, first ever Christmas with snow on the ground and nobody to share it with ... I could go on and on, but I think you get the general drift.'

'Indeed I do. What worries me is how much of that rubbish *you* made up, and how much was just Mummy dear at her scintillating best. And why!'

'Really, Anne. It's quite obvious she rather fancies me as a replacement for your—er—boyfriend.'

Ex-boyfriend, she thought, but didn't—wouldn't!—say it out loud. John's place in her life had evaporated as thoroughly as her job; with any luck she might never see him again, although she knew better than to suspect she wouldn't have to talk to him before her departure, just to clear the air. 'She'd fancy anybody in that role, so don't go getting a swelled head over it,' she replied savagely. 'And you would have aided and abetted, for sure; I remember you saying you wanted to meet her.'

'To *see* her,' he corrected. 'And that only so I can see what you'll look like when you grow up.'

'Like my father, only female,' she said without a second thought. 'You only have to look at the two of us together to see that, so you could have saved yourself the trouble.'

'Well, I can always compare dispositions, then,' said Steele, and laughed at her snarl. 'I'd almost get the impression you don't want me along tonight,' he added. 'Which makes me wonder what it is that you don't want me to learn about you. Does your mother make a habit of bringing out your baby pictures or something?' And he laughed. 'I rather fancy you all naked on a bearskin rug, actually.'

'Not even when I was a baby,' Anne retorted, biting back a more caustic reply that was prompted by the warmth that surged through her loins when *she* thought of him seeing her that way, though certainly not as a child.

The worry was that he might be too accurate, generally, in his assessment of the possibilities. There was, to her certain knowledge, no picture of her naked on a bearskin at any age, but it wouldn't be at all surprising for her mother to dredge up all sorts of remembrances, depending on what role she'd chosen for herself that evening.

Sneaking a sideways glance at Steele, Anne found herself predicting that her mother would take one look at him, then launch into *femme fatale* mode, which

Anne would find quite amusing if it involved anyone else.

In the end, she found it amusing even with Steele, although that was about the only enjoyable part of the visit. They arrived to be greeted effusively while her mother gushingly accepted Steele's gaily wrapped 'gift for the house', a small, elegantly carved bowl of Tasmanian black-heart sassafras that emerged from one pocket of his sheepskin jacket. From that instant, Anne might as well not have been there, and she had moments when she thought her mother actually wished it so.

She was subjected to a carefully staged character assassination so subtle she would have missed it except for the way Steele manipulated her mother's conversation. And then she was simply ignored, and during the dinner—her mother's expectably excellent cooking, liberally spiced with hints about how much work she'd put into it—Anne found herself speculating again about how Steele *must* have come prepared for this. Or did he, she wondered, carry a ready supply of such 'gifts for the house' just on the off-chance that he'd need one?

He would, she realised. It was exactly what he would do, because Steele Murdoch was nothing if not a planner; he always seemed to be one step ahead, no matter what the situation.

And so it proved throughout the meal and the rest of the evening. Steele played up to her mother something shocking, Anne thought. But *she* loved it, seemed to totally thrive on it, shed pounds and even years in the process. If we don't get out of here soon, Anne found herself thinking, my mother's going to be younger than I am. And twice as silly.

But eventually, forced to the background by this meeting of giants, she was able to relax and enjoy the performance for what it was. And to be surprised by the realisation that, while Steele clearly knew he was acting, Anne wasn't quite so sure about her mother. Overall, though, her own role as spectator was quite enjoyable. There was an anxious moment when Steele was invited for Christmas dinner the next day, but he skilfully avoided that trap by pleading an earlier commitment.

'I'm picking up a rental car last thing tonight and I'm driving to Whitecourt to see an old friend of Curtis's,' he claimed. And then, astonishingly, he threw Anne the lifebuoy she'd been praying for, if only subconsciously. 'I had planned to take Anne along, but of course I wouldn't dream of disrupting your plans,' he added.

Anne said nothing; to do so would have been fatal. Nor was it necessary. Even she could see that Steele's charm had totally taken in her mother, who was half in love with the Australian and would convince herself the rest of the way by morning.

What followed was a predictable song and dance in which she insisted that Anne accompany Steele, all the while ensuring that everybody knew what a hardship it would be for her personally, not having her daughter at Christmas dinner.

Anne realised for the first time with total clarity what she'd often thought: that her mother didn't really care what she did, within reason, of course, provided she had ensured that Anne would feel guilty afterwards. She's done it all my life, Anne realised. And the same with Kathleen; the very same. Her other realisation, that her mother was jealous of her—and of her sister—was less solidified, but it was there, and ripening quickly.

'You're being awfully quiet,' Steele said after they'd got halfway back to his hotel without Anne saying a word. 'Did I do something particularly to upset you this evening, or was it just me generally?'

'It wasn't you at all,' she told him, not thinking about being evasive.

Steele didn't reply, instead concentrating on the street and household Christmas lights as they passed them. They were nearly at his hotel when Anne suddenly thought, and said without warning, 'I've just realised that I don't know my mother at all. And I'm not sure *she* does either. She's like an endless chain of one-act plays with a constantly recurring theme—guilt!'

'That's pretty heavy stuff for Christmas Eve,' he remarked very gently, 'although I can't say I'm really surprised.'

'What's that supposed to mean?'

'It means you've probably just seen her for the first time through the eyes of an adult,' he said. 'So instead of reverting instantly and chucking me out in the snow, how about coming up for a Christmas Eve nightcap? We've got to plan tomorrow's expedition anyway, if you're really intending to come along.'

'To Whitecourt? Who does my father know there that you have to see? And on Christmas Day, of all days.'

'Nobody that I know of.'

Anne was so surprised that she almost side-swiped a Mercedes in the hotel parking area.

'You . . . lied?'

He shrugged. 'It was, as you said on the way earlier, better than the alternative. I *have* got a car organised and I *was* planning to spend the day driving around; Whitecourt's on the map I was looking at.'

'But you never lie,' she said, only to realise and be just a touch surprised at how certain of that she was.

He shrugged again. 'I don't usually go around making non-existent plans for people without consulting them either. Tonight, although it's no excuse, really, both measures seemed called for. It seemed obvious to me that you didn't want tomorrow to be a repeat performance, which I'm sure it would have been. If I was wrong, I apologise, and you can say that my plans had to be changed at the last minute or that I've come down with pneumonia or whatever, and go on to Christmas dinner with your family. As you perhaps should. For me, I'm shamed to admit that I couldn't handle a repeat performance.'

Anne didn't know what to say. He'd saved her tonight from what could have been a truly embarrassing situation by diverting her mother's attentions, and he'd saved her—if she wanted that—from what she knew would be a similar situation tomorrow whether Steele was there or not. Kathleen and her family would be a captive audience for Mother to rehash tonight in every gory detail.

'You don't have to thrash it out just this minute,' Steele said, his voice strangely gentle. 'Come on up for a nightcap and worry about it all some other time. This is Christmas, after all; you're supposed to be jolly and enjoy yourself. We might even find a present for you under my tree, if you're lucky.'

'You're right, of course,' Anne said, pleased that one thing had worked out right—she had Steele's present safely tucked in her handbag, a small pewter loon crafted with such delicacy that she could almost hear its haunting call.

Somehow it seemed quite natural but still unexpectedly comforting to have him take her arm as they walked to the hotel entrance, and to have him keep his grip right through the lobby, up in the lift and right to the door of his room. It was a proprietorial grip, but just, tonight, what she needed.

Steele hung up their coats while Anne struggled out of her snowboots and back into the flimsy slingbacks that complemented her dress, thinking as she did so that the dress, barely decorous enough at her mother's, now seemed far more revealing in the intimacy of Steele's hotel room.

Then she straightened up, looked around the opulent room, and forgot her concerns as she gasped with surprise and delight. He did have a Christmas tree! It was only tiny, to be sure, sitting on a little pot on the dresser, but it was a proper tree, and with presents under it as well. He was kneeling to adjust something in the room's sound system, so Anne took the opportunity to tiptoe over and place her present to him under the tree, stepping back just as a soft whisper of Christmas music flowed through the room.

'That's better,' said Steele, straightening up. 'Now let's see about that drink. Piper's Brook, I presume?'

'What else, at Christmas?' she replied, her eyes bright now, feeling relaxed, comfortable, a total change from earlier in the evening. She sank down on to a sofa and accepted the glass when Steele handed it to her, lifting it to meet his own in a toast.

'To...Christmas,' he said softly, his eyes like smoke infused with motes of sunlight. 'And to our journey together next year.'

As they clicked their glasses lightly, then took a first sip of the nectar-like wine, he held Anne with his eyes, touching and caressing her as surely as if she were in his arms. She felt the warmth of that caress matching that of the wine as his eyes followed its path down her throat, then lower.

'Truly beautiful,' he murmured, sipping at his own wine, savouring it just as Anne savoured his compliment, his visual caress.

Then both lapsed into a wondrously peaceful silence, sipping their wine, gazing comfortably at each other and listening to the music. When Steele eventually rose to refill their glasses, Anne shook her head; she still had to drive home.

'Would you like me to send down for some coffee? A snack?'

And disrupt all this tranquillity? 'No,' she replied, her own voice just a whisper against the music. 'I'm fine.'

'Very fine,' he smiled. 'Extremely fine, in fact.' And when he set his glass aside and reached down to take her hand, to lift her upright and into his arms, the whole approach seemed just made for her mood of tranquillity.

His lips tasted of the good wine, his breath was warm and soft against her mouth. Within the circle of his arms, she could feel the heat of his body against her, and even in her high heels she had to stretch to make them fit just so. She wrapped her hands around his neck, feeling the strong muscles, the close-kinked curls of his inky hair.

His lips traced infinite patterns from her mouth, touching her eyes, her cheeks, her forehead, her throat, each kiss a caress, some almost a torment because they didn't last long enough. She wanted to inhale him, devour him, meld with him. His hands traced other, more intimate patterns along the small of her back, music along her spine, different, wilder music as he cupped her buttocks to hold her closer, tighter against him.

Then his kisses slid down her neck to spread warmth across her shoulders, to dip into the valley between her breasts, his mouth pushing aside the flimsy shoulder-straps of the dress to provide new hunting grounds. Her nipples sprang erect to meet his lips, throbbed against the teasing touch of his tongue.

Fingers teased at the back of her dress, then his body shifted only enough so that the dress could spill to a pool of green around her ankles, so that his jacket, then his shirt, could disappear. And now the warmth of their bodies was a liquid, living thing, spilling tendrils of fire along her ribs as he kissed her there, pooling in coals where she felt his arousal against her.

He lifted her, carried her to the enormous bed, laid her down with her arms still coiled round his neck, his lips still chained to her own. And then he was beside her, his lips and hands doing things she wanted, things she had only ever dreamed of. Her own hands were exploring without conscious command, touching, searching, relaying messages to a brain that seemed drugged by his kisses.

If there was a time they could have stopped, Anne never knew it. There was a vague moment when Steele tried to speak, but she didn't want to hear him, didn't want to know. She smothered his words with her kisses, plunged her hands to the very core of his passion, held him silent with quicksilver fingers, with a mouth that wanted only to drink in the very essence of him.

And then there was no stopping; they plunged together into a maelstrom of sensation, a time without sound or logic or meaning in which their bodies became one, in which Anne felt certain she would faint, would explode, would explode from the volcano inside her. She couldn't think, couldn't breathe, could only wonder as it happened, then couldn't even do that.

She came back to sanity with her body tingling to the touch of his fingers stroking in lazy patterns along her body and his voice accompanying them in a soft, barely audible monotone. It was, she thought as she shrugged into his touch, like somebody stroking a cat. She liked being a cat.

'Merry Christmas,' he said, and his voice was melting chocolate.

Anne's reply was as much a purr as anything. She felt as if her bones had melted, as if her entire body was now just one huge pool of sensation, of response to his touch.

'I suppose now you've worked your wicked way with me you're going to leap up and demand your Christmas present?' Teasing melted chocolate now. She smiled at the teasing.

'Isn't that what I just had?'

'Not if it means being limited to once a year,' he smiled. And his eyes were pools of dark warmth, his voice now a caress in itself. His fingers continued their idle stroking, as if to maintain her on the verge of another erotic journey. Anne could only sigh, wriggling with content.

'Only allowed to open one present on Christmas Eve,' she mumbled contentedly. 'I think I've had mine.'

'I know I have,' he chuckled. 'But it isn't Christmas Eve any more. Although,' he said, shaking his head wearily, 'I do hope to get a bit of sleep before facing much more of Christmas Day.'

Anne stretched, luxuriating in that wondrous, boneless feeling. She was already asleep, she thought; surely this had to be a dream. One from which she never wanted to wake.

Steele's hands moved more purposefully now, his lips following before he shifted so that his mouth and teasing tongue could find her lips, part them. Anne's body was moulded like clay in his hands, her skin on fire to his touch. And this time their journey together was slow; he refused to let her dictate the pace, but took her to the edge and kept her there, on fire, until they fell together into a pool from which Anne emerged sated, her mind and body engulfed in a strange lassitude of utter contentment.

'Sleep now,' he whispered, his lips brushing her mouth, then her ear.

She did, and woke, gradually, to the insistent sound of burbling, splashing water. Torpid and disorientated, she lay there, eyes closed, until memory forced them wide awake and she looked over to see Steele lounging, smiling, in the jacuzzi.

'Merry Christmas,' he said, and waved an invitation. 'Come and join me? It's quite splendid, especially if you look out of the window first. It must have snowed all night!'

Her answer was to whisper an uncertain, 'Merry Christmas,' her voice subdued by an onslaught of shyness. She pulled the covers up to her throat, her eyes darting round the room. Her gown had obviously been hung up, along with Steele's clothing, and the rest of her gear was neatly piled on the night table, much as she herself might have done.

But beneath the covers was . . . just her! She pulled the covers in more snugly, shyly looking across to where Steele, obviously wearing no more than she, looked with laughing eyes at her predicament.

'It isn't funny,' she protested, certain she was blushing all over.

'It is, you know. At least from this viewpoint.' And he chuckled wickedly. 'Come and see for yourself; I'll close my eyes until you're safely hidden in the bubbles.'

'*Safely* hidden?' Now it was Anne's turn to laugh. He was right; the whole situation was becoming ludicrous. She flung off the covers and walked across the room towards him, fighting off the desire to lift her hands to try and cover herself. Especially as the merriment in his eyes changed to blatant desire. A hand reached up for her hand as she reached the tub, and she stepped into a whirlpool of warm bubbles to find herself crushed against an even warmer body, fingers that reached out to caress her, lips that sought, and found, her own.

'You promised me safety,' she blustered after being so thoroughly kissed she could hardly breathe.

'I lied.'

All modesty vanished at his touch, and she flowed into his arms, awash now with sensation that seemed heightened by the pulsation of the jacuzzi, the fresh smell of the bubble-bath around them.

'Is this how all executives travel?' she teased. 'Very macho, all this bubble-bath.'

'It's here for you,' he replied. 'And if it's macho you want...' Fingers guided her hand beneath the soap bubbles while his lips reinforced the message. Not that it was required. Anne let herself float into ecstasy as their bodies merged in the pulsating waters.

'I suppose you can wear my dressing-gown,' Steele mused an aeon later. 'You'll have to have something on if they're going to bring us some food, and I'm going to faint with hunger if they don't.'

Now Anne's modesty returned with a vengeance. 'I can't be here when...' she fumbled. Never in her life had she been in such a situation, and she found it suddenly terrifying.

'Well, I suppose you could hide in the closet,' he laughed. 'But I fail to see the logic, considering I'll be phoning down for breakfast for two. Unless you want me down on the hotel's guest list as a glutton.'

'Instead of as a lecher? Or do they already know that? And what about *my* reputation? I suppose that isn't important, so long as you can maintain your macho image?'

'Your reputation is safe as houses,' he replied, laughing. 'They don't even know your name. But maybe you should be hidden in the closet, lest I become categorised as a dirty old man.'

'Which you are,' she retorted, stung just a bit by the implication about her age.

'And loving every minute of it.' He climbed from the bath in a parody of geriatric movement. 'I'll just hobble over and get you that robe, my dear, before I expire,' he croaked.

But when he returned with the robe, himself now clad in jeans and a well-used sweater, Anne made no move to leave the soapy haven of the tub.

'Maybe I should just stay here,' she ventured. 'I only have to duck my head under the bubbles and . . .'

'OK,' he said—too quickly. He was dialling room service even as Anne floundered quickly from the bath and into a towel. She was drying herself briskly even as he was delivering a breakfast order sufficient, she thought, for five people. But when it arrived—to find her snuggled in his robe and carefully tucked into the questionable security of the bed—Anne found herself hungrier than she'd ever have believed. The waiter was barely out of the door when she was sitting across from Steele at the small dining-table, eyeing the food as if it were to be her last meal.

Well worth it, if it had been her last meal, she decided some time later, looking at a tray on which only crumbs remained of the toast and crumpets and bacon and eggs and hashbrown potatoes which had seemed earlier to be far too much. Anne was on her second cup of coffee, Steele on his third.

'That car I ordered should be arriving soon,' he said. 'And since I presume you won't want to be driving in the country wearing what you had on last night, shall I drive you home to change, or follow you?'

'I *ought* to take the Beetle home, I suppose, if I can find it under all this snow,' Anne replied, and suddenly went all shy again as she thought of leaving the hotel at this hour wearing the only clothes she had. Wandering in and out of luxury hotels wearing evening clothes was a totally new experience for her, and she felt distinctly uncomfortable.

'Nobody's going to notice,' Steele grinned, as if once again reading her mind. 'Not even when we get back, because I'll be a gentleman and carry your suitcase for you.'

'Suitcase?'

'Of course. You may want warm clothes for our drive, but I'm sure you'll want something fancy for Christmas dinner; it does call for something a bit more posh than jeans.'

'Christmas dinner... but we've only just had breakfast.' This was going much too fast for Anne, and she wasn't at all certain about the direction.

'We have, and I'm sure we'll have lunch too, at some point,' he said, apparently relishing her confusion. 'But *dinner*, complete with all the appropriate trimmings, we shall be having here, in the dining-room, fashionably late, and suitably dressed. Unless of course you'd rather risk room service? You're going to need *some* clothes, regardless, although hardly on my account.' And his eyes slid down the neckline of his robe, which had slipped open sufficiently that Anne didn't have to guess his meaning.

'For a man who's famous for his planning, you really let the side down this time,' she quipped, pushing herself away from the table and starting for the bathroom to get changed. 'I've half a mind to just leave you here and go home, where things don't happen quite so... so... without any plan at all.'

'I didn't plan this, dear girl,' he told her with a grin that was truly mischievous. 'I just... hoped.'

'I'll bet you did,' she replied. 'And I just hope you're pleased with the result too.'

'Aren't you?'

'I honestly don't know,' she confessed, struggling with her tights. Not entirely true; she was, at best, ecstatic, but by the same token everything was moving much too fast for her to keep up. Did Steele expect her to move in with him? Here? Did their new status as lovers mean they'd be sharing rooms, sharing *beds*, in Los Angeles and Hawaii *en route* to Australia? She slipped into her gown, reached behind her to zip it up, and found another pair of fingers already waiting.

'Let me,' and his lips moved from whispering in her ear to trace a delightful path down her neck to her bare shoulder. Then he turned her to face him, so that he could kiss her properly on the mouth. 'This is all going much too fast for you, isn't it?' he asked, and, without waiting for a reply, 'Would you rather just go home where you can think it all out, and join me for dinner—or not, as you please—later?'

What she really wanted, Anne knew, was to just stay where she was, in his arms, safe and protected. But that was totally unrealistic; she realised with a momentary panic that she still hadn't phoned John's mother to beg out of Christmas brunch. Not something she could do here, not with Steele listening. And she would have to speak to John in the process; that would be even worse!

She even thought of dropping by her mother's to see her sister and her family. They would have arrived by now, would be expecting a call at the very least. Then she found herself imagining the hoo-ha if she walked in wearing the same clothes as last night, and couldn't help but explode with laughter.

'You do have strange ideas, my love,' Steele said, shaking his head after she'd explained. And Anne's tummy did a little back-flip; it was the first time he'd actually said that word 'love', and suddenly she found herself wondering if it meant anything at all. It was a word used too lightly anyway, so common in Australia as to mean anything or nothing at all. She could remember her father commenting that he never bothered to remember names—he could call all the men 'mate' and all the women 'love' and get by quite comfortably. Was '*my* love' so very different?

'I think I will go home,' she decided out loud. 'If you're sure you can find Whitecourt without me, that is. You're crazy as a loon even thinking of driving in this, you know; there must have been three inches of snow last night.'

'Should be all right on the highways,' he replied calmly, so damnably confident. Anne wished *she* could feel such confidence, or at least look as if she did. The trouble was, she didn't! Just the thought of having to leave the hotel, dressed as she was, had her trembling; she'd better go now or she mightn't find the courage.

'If I'm not back in ten minutes, you can presume the old Beetle started all right and you'll see me again at about . . . seven? That's if I don't lose my nerve, of course.'

Steele held her coat for her, taking another opportunity to kiss the back of her neck as he did so.

'You won't lose your nerve,' he said quietly, turning her so that he could kiss her gently on the lips. 'You won't dare! You haven't opened your Christmas present yet—despite several opportunities—so it'll have to be tonight or wait until next year.'

'Just see that you leave *yours* alone until tonight, then,' Anne retorted with a pertness she didn't quite feel. 'I'll be checking, don't forget, so no peeking, no shaking, no fiddling!'

'I opened my favourite Christmas present of all time last night,' he said with yet another gentle kiss. 'Now go, if you really must, before I decide to do it again.'

Taking him at his word, she fled. Feeling so self-conscious that she might as well have been wearing nothing, never mind her bulky sheepskin jacket and knee-high snowboots, she slunk through the spacious lobby like a thief, almost disappointed that nobody seemed to notice her passing, only to have it all come apart when the doorman smiled, wished her Merry Christmas, and offered to sweep the snow off her car. Which he then did, diplomatically keeping his thoughts, now magnified beyond all logic in Anne's mind, to himself.

'So much for anonymity,' she muttered to herself, only just managing to get the cranky little car to start, and half an hour later was parking in front of her apartment building with every one of her inhibitions, all her second thoughts and even some third thoughts alive and well and waiting for her.

So was John!

Dear John—so safe, so predictable, so totally and completely—now—irrelevant. And so very, very angry.

'I came to go with you to Mum's, he said, his eyes taking in every detail of her appearance, reading what he wanted from it, and liking nothing. 'I'll be late now, and you're pretty obviously not coming, I suppose.' Sulky, juvenile, whingeing. The Australians, Anne found herself thinking uncharitably, must have had John in mind when they invented the word.

And irrelevant. 'I'll give you a ride now, if you like,' she offered, 'but I won't be staying except to apologise to your mother. I meant to phone earlier, but . . .'

'Don't bother explaining; I can guess,' he sneered. 'Friend of your father's, eh? Couldn't he wait until he got you back to Australia before he got you in the sack? Or was it you who couldn't wait?'

He was trembling, trying to build up the nerve, Anne realised, to hit her. She stared him down, forced him to step aside as she put her key in the door and opened it.

'I'm sorry, John,' she said. And she was, but only for him. Not that he'd ever need it, she realised; he was too busy feeling sorry for himself to need her help. 'I'll tell your mother you might be late when I phone to apologise,' she said firmly, and closed the door behind her, leaving him in the hall, leaving him entirely.

As she looked round the flat, seeing it as if for the very first time, Anne realised that no matter what happened now, no matter how things worked out between her and Steele Murdoch, she wouldn't be coming back to this flat, wouldn't be coming back to John, might not even—she thought—be coming back to this city, where she'd been born.

She was burning her bridges without even realising she'd lit the match.

CHAPTER SEVEN

'YOU'RE awfully subdued,' Steele said, drawing Anne's attention from where she'd been staring into space, looking across the festively decorated dining-room of the hotel but seeing nothing.

'I'm sorry. I'm just not . . . feeling all that "ho-ho-ho" tonight,' she replied with a forced smile. 'I guess I came down the wrong chimney or something.'

'It wasn't a complaint,' he smiled. 'And you certainly don't look as if you came down any chimney. Most astonishingly beautiful, actually.'

Hardly that, Anne thought. After spending the entire day in a fruitless round of recriminations and wondering, she'd made her decision to join Steele for Christmas dinner almost at the last minute. And then, rushing to get ready and get out of the flat before she changed her mind for the five-hundredth time, she had opted for safety and tradition. The result was a long black skirt topped by a high-necked, long-sleeved shirtwaist in a soft, delicate shade of mauve. The effect was, she hoped, sufficiently dressy for the occasion while still being demure, rather than provocative.

'It's this brooch that's astonishingly beautiful,' she told him, lifting her hand to her Christmas present and looking down at it with a degree of awe. The brooch was a substantial piece of solid Queensland boulder opal, carved—obviously by an expert hand— into a stylised wombat.

The threads and blocks of colour within the dark opal matrix had been taken into account to produce something quite stunningly unique and beautiful. And frighteningly expensive; she'd learned enough about opal during her visit to Australia to know that much!

Across the table from her, resplendent as always in a finely tailored dark suit, his tan shown off to full advantage by the whiteness of his shirt, Steele too had seemed a bit reflective during their superb dinner. Was he too, Anne wondered, having major second thoughts about their Christmas Eve lovemaking?

It wouldn't be surprising, because she certainly was. Even here, now, with him sitting right there across from her in this luxurious dining-room, she could hardly believe it had all happened. In the dinginess of her flat, it had seemed almost totally unbelievable, except for the constant messages from her body.

Unbelievable, yet she could remember every instant, every word, every response. Was it really possible for her to have been so... wickedly abandoned in her responses? To have done what she did, said what she had? To have so thoroughly enjoyed it all? Was sex supposed to be so much *fun*?

She had eventually determined during her day of soul-searching that tonight would see no repeat performance, but over dinner she had found herself seeing Steele not as he was now, but as he'd been the night before. *Late* the night before. And this morning! She found herself having little glimmers of ridiculous fancy, like when she'd picked up her wine glass a moment earlier and thought about tasting the wine from his mouth, in bed, now!

And from the looks she occasionally caught him giving her Steele might well have been having similar thoughts. Anne was glad, momentarily, that she'd thought to wear a bra under the sheer fabric of her shirtwaist. Without it, the evidence of the effect his glances were having would be all too obvious.

If we were having this dinner in his room, she thought with the most delicious wickedness, we'd be lucky to get past the entrée, by anyone's translation. And she tried to hide the smile that suggestion produced.

'You keep doing that,' Steele said with a matching smile of his own, 'but you never reveal what's so funny. Or is it some deep, wicked secret?'

'I was just thinking about giving you another Christmas present.'

The words slipped out even as she thought them, and Anne nearly dropped her wine glass, over which she'd been quietly watching Steele watching her. Had she really said that? She looked down at the table, at first unable to face Steele's equally astonished look, then unable to keep from giggling at it.

'No more wine for you,' he replied after a long silence, then looked at her, wicked speculation in his eyes. 'And no more for me either, if you're serious.'

Not really a question, but there was an unmistakable message there, one that kindled a slow, warm glow in Anne's tummy and spread it down through her loins, making her legs so weak that she knew she couldn't have stood up, just at that moment, if she'd had to.

Worse, she didn't know how to reply. All her good intentions fled before the passion in Steele's eyes; all her reproaches and second thoughts melted in the growing heat between her thighs.

But she couldn't. Wouldn't! Not tonight. She was supposed to be feeling guilty at having deceived her mother, supposed to be feeling—something?—at ending things with John once and for all. His mother, when she'd phoned, hadn't seemed much upset by Anne's last-minute and obviously contrived excuses, Anne found herself recalling, and wondered, Why think of that now?

She met Steele's eyes in silence, her fingers toying with the charm bracelet that held her father's Christmas present—a tiny silver unicorn. Was she serious? Was she even sane? She reached out for her wine glass and emptied it in a single gulp. Let him figure out his own answers, she thought as the waiter saved her by arriving to enquire about their choice of dessert.

'If my mother were to walk in right now, she'd have hysterics,' Anne said in a desperate bid to change the subject. 'She'd kill me, right here on the spot.'

Steele shrugged, his eyes laughing. 'She'd kill *me* if she knew what I was thinking,' he said. 'And she can't be as infallible as you reckon, or she'd have done it last night at dinner too.'

'You weren't thinking about me at all, then,' she laughed. 'You were too busy laying the Murdoch magic charm on Mother. And she was so busy lapping it up I'm surprised she could think at all.'

'Purely self-defence, and you know it,' he grinned. 'Which didn't detract any from my ability to think about you the entire time.'

His eyes were like dark pools, and she looked away for a moment, unable to continue meeting his gaze without having more of those decadent thoughts. Looking down, she realised that he had her hand in his own, that his fingers were gently stroking the inside of her wrist, slowly, deliberately, tantalisingly.

'You have to stop that,' she sighed, not even trying to move the hand. 'Everybody will be looking at us if you keep it up.'

'Everyone?' He looked carefully round the elegant room, and Anne followed his eyes, noting the number of other couples who seemed so totally enthralled with each other that the roof could have fallen down without them noticing.

'Almost everyone,' she replied, nodding to show she'd taken his point. 'Where do all these people come from, I wonder? I . . . I just always think of Christmas as a family occasion; it would never have occurred to me to have Christmas dinner out. It's something you do at home.'

'Only if you're home to do it,' he pointed out. 'And only if you have enough family handy to make it worth the effort. For a lot of people, this is far preferable to being alone.'

'But nobody here *is* alone,' Anne protested. 'They're all couples at the very least, and most of them look anything but lonely.'

'I would have been alone, and I suspect I almost was,' he said with startling perceptiveness. 'And you can be damned well sure I'd have been lonely too.'

'And I wouldn't? If I'd decided not to come, that is. I'd have been having a cheese sandwich instead of all this, too, while *you* would have been lonely in the height of luxury.'

'You could have gone to your mother's.'

Anne laughed. 'And gone crazy trying to re-member which lies I'd told and which ones I'd only thought I'd told about where I'd spent the day and who I'd met and——' She broke off, unable to continue because of chuckles that kept breaking through. Then, 'How was Whitecourt, by the way? You never did tell me.'

'You probably should go to your mother's, if only for coffee or something,' he said, ignoring her question. 'Would you like me to go with you? We can work out our stories on the way, so that we don't contradict each other.'

She looked at him, aghast. 'You're serious,' she said. 'You really want us to drive all the way out there, for a cup of coffee? And fine-tune this wondrous web of deceit while we're on the way? You are amazing.'

'I'm serious when I say that I think *you* should go,' he corrected her. 'I offered to go along because it would let us limit how long you have to be exposed to whatever it is you're so afraid of, and because I'm a better fibber than you are; you, my love, couldn't lie straight in bed.'

'There's nothing at my mother's to be afraid of,' Anne protested. 'Except feeling guilty, of course, but that's nothing new.'

'I should think not.' And there was something in the way he said it that gave her pause, only their desserts arrived just at that moment, so she never got the chance to consider it fully.

But after she'd finished the dessert the thought returned, and she said, 'You're right, as usual. I'm going to feel guilty one way or the other, but it would probably be easier if I did the right thing. It is Christmas, after all. And...'

'And she's your mother and you love her dearly,' Steele added for her. 'You probably should have gone

today, said you overslept and missed me or something, instead of being all alone with your conscience.'

Far too perceptive, Anne thought. Just one more
thing to add to her worries, this uncanny ability he
seemingly had to read her mind, or her moods, or
both. At moments like this she really did feel too
young.

'I will go,' she said with some determination. 'But
alone, I think; there's no reason to subject you to
another of Mother's performances.'

Steele nodded, then said, 'And afterwards?'

'Afterwards,' Anne replied, firm in her resolve, 'I
shall go home.'

And she did, to a virtuous but incredibly lonely bed,
which, if it was supposed to make her feel better, failed
miserably. Her body kept her awake half the night
with physical memories that pleaded and begged to
be repeated, and her mind kept her up the other half
with answerless questions and lashings of mother-
induced guilt.

About the last thing she wanted was to join the rest
of her family in accepting Steele's invitation to spend
the day with him checking out the wonders of 'The
world's largest indoor amusement park', as it was
euphemistically described in the advertising.

'They'll break you,' she'd warned him when he'd
suggested it. 'You've never seen anything like my sister's kids let loose in a place like this. You've just got
no idea what you're letting yourself in for.'

'Oh, yes, I do,' he'd assured her, waving a West
Edmonton Mall brochure in her face. 'If God had
intended *me* to indulge in things like "the Perilous
Pendulum", or "the Stupendous Orbitron"—I
wonder where they get these names from, anyway?

Why call the world's largest indoor triple-loop roller-coaster the "Mindbender"?—he wouldn't have intended children to do it for me! Frankly, the names alone are enough to reduce any sane adult to absolute and utter cowardice.'

'You'd better not be too much of a coward,' Anne had laughed. 'If they get you into the Water Park, you'll be expected to give body-surfing demonstrations and show us the Australian crawl at its scintillating best. And you'll *have* to give a fearless performance on the——' she grabbed the brochure from him '—the "Twister" and the "Screamer" and, if I know my sister's kids, every other one of the twenty-two "high-riding waterslides". The bronzed Ausslie slides again,' she cried. 'Oh, I'm going to just *love* it!'

And she did. Steele, despite his constant referral to them as rug-rats and ankle-biters, truly loved children, and, as Anne knew from her previous visit to Australia, he got along well with them too, treating them as miniature adults and giving serious consideration to the most outrageous proposals.

His response to her sister's two youngsters, and their response to him, was just as Anne expected. He was 'Uncle Steele' within minutes of meeting her five-year-old nephew and four-year-old niece, and had the children planning the entire day for the family before anyone else had a chance to draw breath.

His infectious enthusiasm quickly had everybody involved, driving bumper cars with reckless abandon, screaming with horror and delight on the roller-coaster, cheering as the children conquered the lively carousel ponies. They—being the children, Steele, and more usually both; Anne simply couldn't summon up the courage in many cases—went on every possible ride, tried every possible activity, saw every possible attraction.

Rest periods, of which there were many, allowed the other adults to share in the lashings of popcorn and milk shakes and French fries and candy and gucky, gooey concoctions that Steele said were guaranteed to rot their teeth and who cared? The pace was frantic, hectic, ridiculous, but the children stayed the distance and Steele, like the original Man from Snowy River, was with them at the end.

Anne was exhausted just from watching, her mother was even beaten to a relative silence and the children's parents could only praise Steele for his stamina and deny they'd ever had it.

'The biggest, baddest child of them all,' he bragged as he and Anne sprawled on the sofa in his room, where the two children were sleeping like exhausted puppies on the bed, gathering their strength for an assault on the Water Park. Their parents and grandmother had gratefully accepted the opportunity to 'just sit quietly' for a bit, and Anne wished she could join the children and stay there.

'Aren't they wonderful, the little monsters?' Steele asked in a gargantuan whisper. 'You're exhausted, I'll need a week's sleep to recover from all this, and *they* will be up in about ten minutes ready to do it all again. It's a good thing we're on holiday hours today, or I'm not sure I'd stand the distance.'

But he did, dragging the children and Anne on a marathon tour of the Water Park, where his bronzed, muscular physique and unvarnished enthusiasm drew admiring glances from almost every woman in the five-acre facility.

'Forget about man-made waves and water-slides; give me a man like that any day,' Anne heard one lithesome lass comment to her companion. Both girls were fairly drooling as they speculated on Steele's physical attractions and sexual potential, and she stifled a chuckle as she visualised confronting them to demand a comparison involving who had spent Christmas Eve with whom!

'Unkind, Anne,' she murmured aloud, then laughed as her mother shot her a speculative look across their table in the Tropical Grove, where they were enjoying a drink while Steele was being ogled by every woman within sight.

Anne, snugged into the bikini she'd bought on her Australian visit, was aware of drawing a few admiring glances herself, but the admirers, she thought, paled to mere shadows against the sheer flamboyance of Steele's personality and physical presence. And her mother, never backward about coming forward, made more than one scarcely veiled reference to exactly that. And to the dangers, just generally, of men who were so handsome, so sophisticated, so worldly. Not dangers to Anne, mind you, much less any specific reference to Steele. Just . . . generally. She'd heard it all before, but now it seemed as if she was hearing with new ears, a new perception.

Her mother, Anne was beginning to see, had a tendency to try and poison anything she couldn't control. A little drop here, another drop there, always delivered subtly, almost delicately. And, with the poison, even more frequent drops of guilt. She controlled by guilt, manipulated with guilt. For her, it seemed, loving and being loved was evidenced almost exclusively by guilt.

She hadn't wanted Anne to go to Australia the first time, even less wanted her to go this time. But she would never say so, nor even hint at anything that simply, that directly.

'You'd be well advised to camouflage your feelings a bit, Anne,' her sister whispered across the table during one of the few moments they were alone. 'Apart from the fact that it never does to make things too obvious, you're setting yourself up for a bad time with Mum.'

'Frankly, I don't think it's all that much of her business,' Anne replied. 'And surely to goodness she'd consider Steele a massive improvement over John.' Which, she thought, wasn't really the point. Comparing the two, man and boy, was like trying to compare apples and oranges. There simply was no comparison.

'Don't be too sure,' was the surprising response. 'If the worst came to the worst, she could have controlled John; there's no way known to man she could even think of doing that with this fellow. And she couldn't manage her usual trick of making you feel guilty about the whole thing either, because he wouldn't stand for it.'

Anne had no reply to this unusual sisterly confidence. She wanted desperately to enquire if Kathleen had suffered similar problems early in her own relationship, but couldn't find the words, couldn't formulate the questions without revealing more than she wanted to about her own fears. Luckily, or maybe not so luckily, their mother returned before the conversation could continue.

'I certainly hope they're going to feed you better at your father's than they did the last time,' her mother sighed, eyeing Anne's too slender figure and conveniently forgetting that she'd lost all the weight after her return, not during her visit with her father. 'I suppose this Frenchwoman cooks all sorts of cordon bleu and *nouvelle cuisine* meals that look wonderful but don't give you any sustenance.'

'I don't think anybody considers wallaby stew to be either fancy or without sustenance, Mother,' Anne replied. 'Monique is a wonderful cook, and if I'm there long enough I'm hoping this time she'll be able to teach me a few things.'

'*I* would have taught you to cook, if you'd ever showed any interest,' her mother declared with a sniff of distinct disapproval. Anne remembered a number of so-called cooking lessons during her younger days, when experimentation had been forbidden and her mother had inevitably taken over almost from the beginning to ensure that no mistakes were made. Just another example, she found herself thinking, of her mother's wish to clip her wings and keep her under control.

She bit back a reply that would have caused more problems than solutions, and was saved by Steele's returning at that moment with two fully sated, obviously worn-out children.

'That's it, I think,' he grinned, returning them to their mother with an exaggerated air of relief. 'Which is just as well, because I am fair...ly...rooted.' And he shot Anne—the only one present who might be expected to understand the rude Australianism—a mischievous grin. 'Well, almost, anyway,' he added, and his grin was more than just mischievous now; it was downright wicked.

Anne shook her head in exasperation. He'd been overdoing the use of Australian slang, especially in her mother's presence because he knew she didn't understand the double meanings and would never deign to admit it. But this time it was, she knew, directed entirely at herself. Using the term as a euphemism for exhaustion was one thing; what he was implying now involved sexual exhaustion, and they both knew it.

'Come on, Wombat. Let's see if we can manage just one more decent splash before they shut this place down for the day,' he said, rising to catch Anne's wrist and lift her to her feet. She could have refused, but it would have had to be a verbal refusal, because his grip was like iron. And his eyes said he'd be unlikely to accept her words anyway.

Anne was far too conscious of his muscular, tanned body as he held her close against him, walking the perimeter of the huge wave pool to where the crowds were thinner and they could swim relatively undisturbed. Then he unceremoniously shoved her over the side and dived in to surface with his hands cradling her waist.

'You want feeding up just a bit,' he laughed, and she could only return the laugh, thinking of what her mother had said only moments earlier.

'Christmas is barely over and you're complaining about your present already,' she quipped. 'I suppose next you'll be wanting an exchange or a refund.' It was a light and frivolous way of not quite asking what she really wanted to ask. What did he want? What did he expect of her now, with their journey and its enforced closeness ahead of them?

Her answer was a sudden change in those dark, deep eyes, an expression that she couldn't read, couldn't understand. And wasn't going to be allowed to, she realised.

'We've got a long way to go before you have to worry about that,' he said enigmatically, holding her close against him beneath the water, forcing her to feel their closeness and its effect on him. And on her! Anne couldn't deny the sheer physical reactions he could create in her just with a touch, a smile, and unquestionably by doing this.

'This is *not* the place,' she snapped, trying in vain to free herself, to put at least *some* distance between them. 'My mother's just over there, you great fool.'

'And wishing she was over here, instead of you,' he replied without slackening his grip. 'That's half her problem, you know. She's jealous as hell of both you and your sister.'

'Don't be silly,' Anne said, fighting back the warm, hollow feeling inside her. This was madness, carrying on such a conversation while knowing he could take her, here and now, that he wanted to. That she wanted him to! She leaned in against him to give herself room to move, then suddenly splashed water up into his face and thrust herself away to where she could just touch the bottom. She continued to splash him, keeping him at bay, but only just.

'It's hardly a cold shower,' he laughed, returning the splashing, 'but better than nothing, I suppose.' Then his eyes turned serious, piercing into her own. 'You seem to be having an awful lot of second thoughts about all this, Anne. Not planning to change your mind and stay safe in the nest after all, by any chance?'

'I ... I said I'd go with you and I will,' she said, suddenly totally, completely unsure of herself. There had been, in all of this, no commitment from Steele, no declaration of love, no hint of where they would go from here. Had she even any right to expect more? she wondered. Maybe in his world there wasn't any ... more.

And yet ... he was so extremely good with children. Good with everyone, come to that, but especially with children. Flummoxed for words, eager to avoid the seriousness of his probing, she quickly changed the subject to tell him so.

'Hah! Monique's often said we should have half a dozen,' he said. 'Not so likely before, but now that circumstances might be changing ...'

She heard no more. The bottom dropped out of her world with just those few words, and she fled, shutting down her ears by the simple expedient of sinking into the silence of the water around her.

Now that circumstances might be changing! Now that her father was dying, now that Steele and Monique could finally get their act together without the inconvenience of a divorced husband to get in their way! Anne felt sick, felt like gulping in huge quantities of water to still the pounding noise in her head, in her entire being. She wanted to drown, to just die. But first she had to escape.

Kicking out, directionless at first, she swivelled away under the waves, her legs pumping furiously to let her slide otter-like through the crowds. When she came up for air, she didn't bother to look around, simply gasped sufficiently to fill her distressed lungs and kept going, going.

She swam until she thought her lungs would burst, weaving between the other people, fleeing in a patternless route that finally allowed her to emerge from the enormous pool far from where Steele was still visible, looking round as if confused.

By the time he too emerged, Anne had herself under control, was busily drying her hair, her face concealed in the big towel, her trembling no longer obvious but her heart thumping inside her like some soundless drum.

'You got out in a helluva hurry.' Steele's voice was only slightly muffled by the brisk towelling. Anne kept her face covered, managed to mutter her reply without having to look at him, without daring to.

'Cramp,' she lied. 'Sudden—frightened me. Gone now.' Gone as she wished she could be gone, but that, she realised, could not be so. She was committed to going with Steele to Australia, committed to visiting her father—more committed now than she'd been before. He would certainly need her now.

She finished towelling her hair, forced herself to meet Steele's concerned gaze, to see past it to the devious, deceitful person he really was.

'I . . . I think I must have swallowed some water—too much,' she stammered. 'I have to go.' And fled, sure-footed despite her inner turmoil, to the safety of the women's locker-room, where she would surely have broken down but for the presence of both her mother and sister, already changing to their street clothes.

'You look as if you've seen a ghost, Anne,' her mother cried, forcing Anne into a repeat of the lie, but fortunately giving her time to flee this audience, too, into the questionable sanctuary of the toilets.

They were gone when she emerged, and she was able, finally, to face the mirror, the reality, and to emerge into the real world with no sign, she thought, of the trauma she felt inside.

CHAPTER EIGHT

STEELE seemed to have accepted Anne's decision to avoid a repeat of their Christmas lovemaking, despite her occasional earlier teasing. Or perhaps just now he was simply too tired after his exhausting day with the children.

At the very least, he showed no reaction when she voiced plans to return to her mother's house with the rest of the family after their day's outing had ended.

Certainly, she thought, he couldn't see inside her head, couldn't see the real thoughts that governed her decision—and would continue not to do so throughout their journey together and beyond!

She shrugged off his apparent concern about her 'cramps', making light of the situation except to say that she now felt a touch queasy. A touch? Small word to describe the giant, hollow emptiness, vaster by far than the five-acre Water Park, that now comprised her insides.

Damn Steele anyway! And damn herself too, she thought, for being so stupid as to believe he could feel anything significant for her with Monique's sultry, sophisticated beauty awaiting him. She herself had been nothing more than a convenience for him, and a means of salving his conscience while he waited to formalise his affair with her father's wife. Pay for her to visit her dying father, so that he and Monique might feel less like vultures as they waited for him to die.

And have all his creature comforts on the way! Damn
him straight to hell!

What did he expect to do with her *en route* to
Australia? she wondered. He'd pass her off as some
sort of niece, no doubt, giving hotel and restaurant
staff a knowing, man-of-the-world wink that said
everything and nothing at the same time. Well, let
him. She would go to Australia with him, *had* to go
with him if she wanted to go at all. And she did! Just
speaking to her father on the telephone had spurred
her own conscience, freeing feelings she hadn't known
existed. He was, after all, her father! Ill, perhaps; his
dying maybe more of a certainty. But this utter and
faithless betrayal by his friend and his wife . . . that
was too much even for Anne's simple, unsophisti-
cated moral code.

Steele had also accepted her vague reply concerning
when he would be seeing her again. Here, at least,
she was on fairly safe ground; even he must accept
that she needed to sell off her car, vacate her flat—
but please, please, not until the last possible
moment!—and arrange for storage of what she neither
took with her nor got rid of entirely.

Mother, of course, would see to that problem, had
even offered to keep the car if necessary. It would
only be for six months at most, since that was all
Anne's tourist visa was good for. But Anne had
insisted it must be sold, although not telling anyone
that its meagre returns would have to be added in to
the money she had to save to pay Steele back. Now,
more than ever, she *must* repay that debt, she thought,
to free herself of him forever.

The fire of her outrage at how Steele and Monique
were manipulating her kept her going during the next

few days, hectic days in which she advertised the car, negotiated like a bazaar merchant to rid herself of her flat on *her* terms and to *her* convenience.

She did see Steele, of course, had lunch with him one day and dinner the next. But by this time she had sorted out her head and was determined to play the game his way now—only by her *own* rules. The hardest part was when he changed the rules without telling her.

'You want to make application for permanent resident status now, from here,' he said when her passport arrived with its tourist visa all approved. 'You can use your mother's address and arrange for things to be forwarded if necessary.'

'But . . . I hadn't planned to stay in Australia permanently,' she replied without thinking. Of course she hadn't. She was going to see her father through his health crisis, perhaps his dying, but not to stay there. Most especially not now.

Her response caused Steele to glance at her with a most peculiar expression in his eyes, but he only said, 'You might change your mind, might at least have to stay longer than your tourist visa allows. At least this way you'll have started the paper trail from the right end. They don't much like permanent residence applications from tourists after they're already in the country, even on a family reunion basis.'

Confused, but seeing some of his logic, Anne dutifully filled out the forms he provided for her. Her father might well need her for more than six months, she realised suddenly, might need her for quite some time.

Determined as she was to keep from rocking the boat, to keep their relationship at least appearing to be friendly, she found it very hard going some of the time. Steele was too perceptive, too damned perceptive, where Anne was concerned. But she was determined, and whenever he asked if she was feeling all right, or if she was suffering a change of heart, or if she was concerned about any aspect of their imminent journey, she managed to fob him off with some excuse. She was nervous, yes. Or she was having hassles with her mother over some small thing. Any excuse, she reckoned, was better than none, was better than having to tell Steele the truth—that she now knew about him and Monique, and despised both of them for it.

But it was hard, especially now that even she noticed he was, while still totally attentive, more and more accepting her own remoteness. He touched her less, kissed her less often even when the kiss was more a politeness than the raging, passionate kisses of Christmas. If she wanted him to keep his distance, he seemed to be saying, he would do so.

The worst part was that she kept forgetting herself. She was so used to being comfortable in Steele's company, so used to his courtly manners, his decisive way of doing things and his undeniable charm that she sometimes slipped into what she now thought of as the way things were before.

He was still, he said, evaluating the gigantic West Edmonton Mall, looking at every aspect of its performance and seeking to determine if such a thing would work in Australia. Just where in Australia he never got round to telling her, but she reasoned that if such a facility could work in a city the size of Edmonton it might be just as workable in Sydney or Melbourne.

And part of this evaluation seemed to involve trying to test every restaurant, visit every single one of the advertised eight hundred shops and services. And whenever Anne could be coerced into joining him he made a point of asking her opinions, even, she thought with some surprise, of actually listening to them!

It was a never-ending production. More than two hundred fashion shops for women, something like thirty-five menswear shops, shoe shops by the dozen, eleven major department stores. And Steele obviously intended to see each and every one. Not that he made it into a marathon, or a route march. Whenever Anne was with him he seemed to approach the task with a light-hearted gaiety, a total and typically Steele form of irreverence.

'I wonder if we started right at opening tomorrow we could manage to taste just one thing from each of the fast-food outlets?' he said one day—remarkably, right in the midst of a truly gigantic dinner at the Cafe Orleans oyster bar.

'How can you even think of such a thing *now*? There are——' she glanced at one of the various brochures they both seemed to be consulting constantly '—more than fifty pure fast food outlets in this place, and that's not counting the other twenty or so they've listed as "sweets and treats". Here we are, sitting here at the end of a veritable banquet, and you want to think about junk food? You're mad.'

'It isn't all junk food,' he retorted. 'I quite fancy some of the stuff on offer. Some of the Asian food is quite remarkable, considering it's being dished up as fast food. About the only thing generally I'm not fussed about is the hamburgers.'

'Says he who comes from a place where a hamburger isn't real unless it's got beetroot on it!' Anne scoffed. 'I'm not surprised; you wouldn't know a proper hamburger if it jumped up and bit you.'

'You're obviously not impressed with my idea at all,' he replied—quite unnecessarily. 'So what do you reckon we check out all the "sweets and treats" places one by one?'

'And you could buy extra seats on the plane, because we'd need them,' Anne said with a shake of her head. He could be quite ridiculous sometimes. 'I know you think I'm a bit skinny, but really...'

'I think you're just about exactly right,' he put in with a hungry, speculative look that stopped just short of being a leer. 'Not that I've seen enough of you lately to be sure...'

Anne ignored the suggestiveness. There was nothing else, she thought, that she could do. If she opened that subject up for discussion, it would be sure to get out of hand one way or another, and she didn't want any more problems than she already had.

'I have a better idea,' she said brightly. 'Let's go skating. We've hardly even stopped to watch the activities at the Ice Palace, much less tried them out.'

'And with damned good reason, too. My aged and brittle bones aren't up to the risk,' he replied. 'Besides, ice-skating is hardly destined to become a great goer in Australia.'

'It is so. There's a proper skating rink in Hobart; I remember! And I'll bet they exist in Sydney and Melbourne too. You're just afraid I'll show you up, that's all.'

'I'm not afraid of it, but it is a fair assumption you'd do exactly that,' Steele laughed. 'Considering

I've never been on ice-skates in my life. You could probably skate before you could walk.'

'Not quite. Although I did take figure-skating lessons for a while when I was...younger.' Much younger, she suddenly realised, and wondered what she was letting herself in for. Especially when Steele fairly beamed, and voiced an alternative idea.

'Wonderful! You can get rigged out in one of those winter-weight tutu things and strut your stuff; I'll stay here where it's warm and just watch.'

'Not a chance! If I go, you go. If we pick our time right, like just after hockey practice, there should be enough rugged hockey players around to help pick you up when you fall.'

'As I most assuredly will,' he sighed. 'But OK, let's give it a go. Actually, I went roller-skating once or twice when *I* was younger, so maybe it won't be too bad. But you have to promise to nurse me if I wreck myself and have to fly horizontal in a stretcher.'

'That,' Anne replied caustically, 'is what God invented air hostesses for.'

It was no consolation at all, twenty minutes later, to find that Steele's superb co-ordination and reflexes allowed him to become a more than adequate skater in literally minutes. He had a few near-misses, to be sure, but he was partnering Anne in simplified ice-dancing routines long before she was ready for such antics. And, surprising as his agility was, the real surprise was just how intimate it was possible to be in the midst of a huge skating rink filled with a myriad other people.

Throughout, she was constantly aware of his touch, of the way his hands felt as they skated hand in hand, of the way he so easily lifted her, so neatly spanned her narrow waist with his sensitising fingers.

And when it was over, when he was unlacing her skates just as she remembered some boy doing during her impressionable teenage years, Anne wondered how she could have been so silly as to forget just how romantic skating together could be. As she sat there, Steele kneeling before her, she could have kicked herself for even suggesting it all.

And Steele, ever-sensitive, ever-aware of her thoughts, it seemed, looked up and said, 'Maybe we ought to go book shopping now, and I could carry your books for you.' His eyes danced with mischief as he teased her, but it only made Anne wonder if all her deception was really working at all.

It would have been vastly easier, she thought as the days passed in what should have been an idyllic holiday before their long journey, if Steele weren't in such a position of control. Her car was sold; nothing would do but that she should take his rental car, a vehicle she felt almost certain hadn't been used more than once since his arrival. Still, it was unarguably handy, especially as he practically insisted she continue to perform as his companion while he prowled the Mall in search of...whatever. And she'd got better than her expected price for the car, which was also a bonus, she thought. It would make it somewhat easier to pay him back for the air tickets eventually.

That perception lasted right to the last minute, the moment they said goodbye to her mother and boarded the aircraft for the first leg of their journey.

Anne had expected the prices to have gone up since her trip two years before, and had vaguely planned for that. But she hadn't expected—hadn't even dreamed—that Steele would have booked himself, and therefore Anne with him, *first class* all the way!

'It's too long a trip to fly cattle-car if you don't have to, and we don't,' he said as she involuntarily halted in the middle of the aisle, almost trembling as her mind tried to calculate the difference in prices she would now have to consider.

'I...I'm sorry,' she apologised, sliding into her designated seat—the window-seat, of course; trust Steele to arrange that. 'It's just that I hadn't... expected this.'

'That's all right, then,' he grinned, sliding into the seat beside her and reaching out to take her fingers in his own. 'I thought for a minute there you were going to go all bourgeois on me and worry about your middle-class image. We can always go back and find somebody to come up and play gin rummy with you, if that's what you want.'

Anne bristled at the suggestion, mostly because she knew very well that neither she nor Steele was remotely class-conscious one way or the other. He was deliberately stirring, and she wondered why. If he'd intended to explain, he didn't bother now.

'You do realise,' he said instead, 'that we may have to turn around and go back immediately because we forgot something.'

'You may have; I very definitely did not,' she replied, hoping she sounded a great deal more certain than she felt, even more hoping she was right!

'But we did. After all the time we had, we never did get round to seeing every movie that was showing in—what was it—nineteen movie theatres? How could we ever have forgotten that?'

'Self-preservation,' said Anne without hesitation. 'If we had, we'd not only have square eyes by now, but we'd certainly have seen every movie that will be offered during our flights.'

'Exactly what I was hoping,' Steele said with a disarming grin. 'Whereupon we could have spent the entire time canoodling under an airline blanket. Isn't that a wonderful word—canoodling? Conjures up all sorts of lovely images.'

'I do wish you'd stop teasing,' she snorted, unsure whether to laugh or cry at this blatant attempt to put her at ease. 'Can't you ever take *anything* seriously?'

Steele hardly hesitated. 'All right, we'll be serious if that's your preference. Am I correct in assuming— and I can ask this now that it's over—that you really weren't all that fussed about the world's largest indoor shopping centre, otherwise known as "The Eighth Wonder of the World", which certainly says something about Western society?'

'And nothing good either,' Anne replied. 'But to answer your question—no, I'm not all that fussed. You mightn't have noticed, but by far the majority of people in the place, even through the Christmas period, weren't locals. I'm sure there wouldn't be many Edmontonians who haven't been there, and probably more than once, although you hear hardly anybody admit it. But that place wasn't designed for Edmontonians. Edmonton just happens to be where it *is*. It could just as easily be in Calgary or Vancouver or Sydney, for all the difference it makes.'

'What you're saying is that it isn't just a massive shopping centre; it's a tourist attraction. But of course that's the purpose of the exercise, isn't it?'

'I suppose so,' she agreed. 'But it's just too big for me. Maybe because I'm not a tourist in my own city, and certainly because I'm not one of the world's great shoppers. After all, you can only wear so many clothes, only find room for so many ornaments, or paintings, or... well... whatever. Except books, of course! When I'm rich, I'll have rooms and rooms and rooms of bookshelves and spend all my time scrounging in second-hand bookshops.'

Steele smiled at that, as she'd expected he would. He too had a great love of books; she could still remember the oaths he'd voiced when the Tasmanian government forced cutbacks in library services.

Then he shook his head, almost sadly, Anne thought.

'You're really going to hate Hawaii, then,' he said. 'At least the only part of it we're going to have time to see this time around, which is good old Honolulu, the shopper's paradise. It's nothing much more than the West Edmonton Mall multiplied a thousand times and with the roof off it. In fact I'm sure the big Ala Moana centre was touted as the world's biggest shopping centre until they built the Mall in Edmonton; now it's just the biggest "outdoor" shopping centre. But the concept's the same, and, as you said, it's really only just for the tourists. Locals know where they can get what they want for less money, with less hassle.'

'Well, *you* should be right at home there, then,' Anne said with a flash of insight. 'Because you *do* love to shop; I've watched you.' And she laughed with delight at the realisation. 'You do! You didn't drag me through every single shop in the West Edmonton Mall because you were evaluating the concept—you did it because you *loved* it! You did!' And she laughed even louder, only dimly aware that her own over-wrought emotions were forcing her laughter, that she was just as likely to break into tears in a moment.

'Well, you don't have to tell everybody,' Steele growled. 'Think, woman! Suppose there's a Hawaiian businessman on this plane? He'd be out with the sample cases before they even start dishing out the plastic food. And we haven't even got to Los Angeles yet, let alone Hawaii!'

Which, Anne thought, would be a blessing. Trying to be serious with Steele was just as wearing as putting up with his totally irreverent sense of humour. What she really wanted to do was just get this trip over with, get to where she could be with her father and maybe, just maybe, *not* have to be with Steele.

Steele, whose continual touching, taking her hand in his, patting her on the knee, reaching up to brush away a tendril of hair from her cheek, would be just so wonderful if it only meant anything. It felt so wonderful even though she knew it really didn't mean anything. Even though she didn't want it to!

She did her best to force her mind to turn off, and managed well enough that she was able to actually enjoy the rest of the first part of their trip. And there wasn't a long enough delay in Los Angeles for her to have much time to think; they had to scurry just to make the connection, because their plane was a few minutes late and there was some confusion over the baggage.

But they were hardly airborne again when Steele picked up on the subject Anne least wanted to continue talking about.

'Of course if you don't want to shop in Hawaii, or dip your dainty little toes in the waters of Waikiki

Beach along with fifty thousand other tourists, we could always find something else less ... public to occupy our time. The purpose of the stopover is, after all, to rest.'

And he gave her the benefit of a hugely magnified leer to prove he wasn't serious. Only he was, Anne knew, or would be if she showed the slightest interest. His touches might look innocent, but her body knew. Her body knew only too well, she thought. If she wasn't careful that very same body would reveal the interest for her, and then ... No, she determined, she would not think about that.

She found herself asking, 'I suppose you've taken great care to provide for all this *rest*? I don't suppose you'd care to give me a bit of warning about just what's expected of me? Like am I to be chained to the bed, awaiting your convenience? Or have you booked a place with cooking facilities, so I can tend to that too?'

Nasty questions in a nasty tone of voice, but Anne didn't care. If she didn't get Steele at a distance and keep him there, she knew, she might as well give it up; he was so difficult to hate, even when she worked at it.

She sensed, rather than felt, Steele's withdrawal. He didn't release her hand, which she realised he'd been holding for quite some time. Nor did he even look at her directly. In her own peripheral vision Anne could see the strong muscles along his jaw clench and then unclench, saw him close his eyes, reach up with his free hand to rub at them, as if he was in pain. And for what seemed a very long time he said nothing, nothing at all.

And she couldn't stop. Like her laughter, this obsessive needling just kept coming out of her mouth, spurred by her pain and confusion.

'Aren't you going to say anything? I mean, surely my little sexual performances are part of the bargain, aren't they? You must expect *something* for your money, even if I *will* pay back every cent. Or am I losing my appeal, now that you've tried out the merchandise?'

Still silence, still no direct eye contact to indicate if she was getting to him or not. Anne didn't care; she was angry, she was hurt, and she was suddenly very, very tired. Tired of holding it all in, of trying to be somebody she wasn't, of feeling about Steele the way she did, the way she couldn't *not* think of him, no matter what the provocation. And he wouldn't even fight, the bastard!

The arrival of a hostess to take their drink orders saved him this time. The pause, the change of thinking, her instinctive need to avoid making a public spectacle of herself—although she would make one of *him* if she could manage it without her own involvement, she thought—all contributed to a quick calming on Anne's part. And a drink would help too. She opted for a double brandy, which she knew would almost certainly put her to sleep, give her a chance to sort herself out before they landed in Hawaii and she had to face whatever arrangements Steele *had* made.

Those arrangements, to both her pleasure and suspicious disbelief, turned out to involve a two-bedroom suite in a modern and very up-market hotel. Anne had indeed slept during the flight, the brandy combining with her hypertension to put her out like the proverbial log. She'd awakened only when Steele had gently whispered that she must, that they'd be landing soon in Hawaii.

'Wake me when it's over,' she'd sighed, not wanting to wake up, not wanting to face what had to come, yet knowing there was little real choice. By the time they'd cleared Customs and Immigration and answered the questions a bored official insisted on them answering, Anne was wide awake and getting more apprehensive by the minute.

And now—this. A room to herself, with—as Steele bluntly pointed out—a door she could lock. Anne didn't know whether to be relieved or indignant. Steele's attitude didn't help at all. He was the soul of politeness, courteous, pleasant, but . . . cold. Icy cold. Hardly surprising, she thought, remembering with a sort of shame the way she'd acted, the things she'd said.

'I have some things to do,' he advised almost as soon as the bellboy had been despatched with a substantial tip. 'You'll probably want a wander round, in which case I suggest you stay in the main shopping areas and try not to get lost. If you don't want to go out, I can fully recommend the room service here.'

His entire attitude, let alone the ice cubes in his voice, registered dismissal, almost total indifference. He wasn't trying to start a fight, wasn't trying to do anything, Anne thought, except to separate himself from her. Which, she told herself after he'd left, was . . . deserved.

It bothered her while she took a quick shower, then changed into a lightweight blouse and shorts and went out on the balcony to look down into the well-lit canyons of downtown Waikiki. It bothered her even more when, bored and annoyed because it was bothering her, she decided to go out and explore.

She emerged into the sultry, muggy, tropical night air and almost found it hard to breathe, the scent-laden air seemed so heavy. And the crowds! Even at this time of night—it was now nearly eight o'clock, local time—the streets absolutely thronged with people. People in groups, people in pairs, people in couples. About the only people moving about singly, she noticed, were obviously and unmistakably local.

'Except me,' she muttered, and suddenly felt lonelier than she ever had, far lonelier than she'd felt on her first visit to Australia, even lonelier than she had on her way home again, when she'd really been betwixt and between about her feelings for her father, for Steele, for almost everything.

Here I am, in what's probably the second most famous honeymoon destination for all of Canada and half the US, and look at me, she thought, missing Steele's company horribly and angry at herself because she did. After half an hour of wandering, carefully taking note of her route because already the shop windows all looked the same, the shoals of Japanese tourists seemed to ebb and flow with no real sense of direction, no sense of purpose, she decided she'd had enough.

She found her way back to the hotel, dragged out the book she'd not finished during the flights, and sat beside the air-conditioner, reading the same page over and over. If only Steele hadn't been so...so callous about him and Monique having children; if he'd even been straight with her in the beginning, before Christmas Eve; if only she could accept that by comparison to her stepmother she was...

There just isn't any comparison, and you should be old enough to face up to that, she told herself. You asked for everything you got on Christmas Eve—asked for in Australia the first time, for goodness' sake—and now you're whingeing like . . . like John. You're a fool, Anne. Nothing but a fool.

All of which made her feel not one bit better as she finally lay in her bed, unable to sleep, unable to concentrate on anything but the sound of Steele's return, whenever that might be. She eventually fell asleep without hearing him come in, and woke to the certainty that she just had to do something, whatever it might be, to make the rest of this journey at least bearable. Another day of Steele's icy politeness, especially here in Hawaii and regardless of the fact that she herself had provoked it, was just . . . not . . . on, she decided.

The door to his room was closed as she crossed to the bathroom to shower and prepare for whatever the day might offer. It was still dark outside, or as dark as a city that never seemed to sleep could be! Even at this ungodly hour the streets thronged with traffic. And already hot, she found as she poked her nose quickly through the balcony door.

She showered, washed her hair and twisted it, still damp, into a makeshift ponytail, and emerged from the bathroom wearing shorts and the lightest shirt she owned. Steele's door was still closed. Was he even in there? she wondered. Or had he found other, more satisfactory, sleeping arrangements? The temptation to peek was overpowering, irresistible.

And there was no satisfaction, she found to her dismay, in finding Steele's bed empty, obviously having been that way since their arrival. She stood in the open doorway, feeling quite ridiculously angry and chagrined, yet wanting to cry because she also felt so abandoned.

'With nobody to blame but yourself, you stupid woman,' she muttered, flinging herself out of the doorway, slamming the door in frustration, and plunging out on to the balcony to stare blindly out over the beach as dawn bathed the scene in warm, welcoming colours. After a time she returned indoors, tried once again to concentrate on her book, failed, found herself hungry and only managed to dither over whether to order something from room service, which might mean having to face Steele in an uncertain mood, or get herself out of this, at least for now, by seeing if she could find breakfast somewhere else. Cowardice won.

Half an hour later she was sitting in a Denny's overlooking the beach, dithering over the most astonishing breakfast menu and thinking that Steele, as usual, had been right. The Americans certainly could do breakfasts!

Even on a full stomach, she couldn't quite convince herself to return to the emptiness—or worse—of the hotel room, so she set out to walk the beach, instinctively seeking a solitude that seemed impossible on streets already filling with tourists.

She headed for the remotest area she could find, way up past the zoo and towards the aquarium. Ignoring the heat, ignoring the occasional other person she encountered, she simply put her mind into neutral and walked and walked. Then she turned round and walked back again, this time with slightly more determination and a lot less energy; coming into this heat out of full winter, she realised too late, required acclimatisation. But at least she now had a plan. She would force herself to do her best to be civil, even friendly to Steele. She would not only endure the remainder of their journey, she would enjoy it! Somehow.

Back in the shopping district, she found things even more crowded, and with a headache looming—fool, not to have worn a hat, she thought—she debated seeking the shortest, quickest way back to the relative sanctuary of the hotel. She was almost there when a window display caught her eye and a second look caught her sense of humour.

It mightn't be the perfect peace-offering, she thought as she emerged a few minutes later with a parcel beneath her arm, but at least it showed faith—after a fashion.

Whether Steele would agree . . . well, she'd have to wait for his return to see about that. With any luck, she thought, he might have returned already. If not, she could only test one of her few remaining virtues—patience.

Patience wasn't all she'd need, she found when she opened the suite and found Steele still missing. Or, more correctly, missing again; she found a note by the telephone indicating that he had come back to the hotel, if only briefly.

The note was equally brief.

'Fishmonger's Wife. Ala Moana. 12:30.'

No greeting, no 'good morning', no 'how are you?' Much less any question such as 'Would you like to come for lunch?' Anne looked at it, then fought down her anger and suspicion and checked her watch. She might just make it on time.

Only to be thoroughly, totally, exasperatingly confused when she entered her own room and found a gaily wrapped parcel perched on her pillow, with yet another note.

This one was slightly less cryptic.

'I don't know what I've done to upset you. Obviously something quite horrid. This is a peace-offering.'

Anne ripped open the package to find the most wonderful silken sarong, delicately hand-painted in hues that mingled every shade of tropical greens and purples. For her hair colouring—perfect. It was so diaphanous she could enclose it in her hand, and when she stripped and tried it on—it simply pleaded for that—it seemed even more sheer.

'I hope he doesn't expect me to wear this to lunch,' Anne told the slender figure in the mirror, 'because he'll be in for a sad disappointment. This wasn't made for wearing in public.'

She found herself thinking about the T-shirt emblazoned with 'BORN TO SHOP', then shook her head and deposited it on Steele's pillow anyway. He'd either like it or he wouldn't, she determined; at least it was a gesture, however incomparable with his.

Anne was studiously surveying the Ala Moana directory, Steele's first note in her mind, when she suddenly realised that she might have totally misinterpreted it. There was no reason at all to presume the note had even been meant for her; it might be no more than a memo from Steele to himself, a note of a luncheon engagement with *anybody*.

'Now what do I do?' she muttered to herself. 'If he's expecting me and I don't turn up, I'm in the wrong, but if he's merely arranged lunch with somebody else and I do show up... What if it's somebody I'm not supposed to meet in the first place?'

Deciding she could—and probably would—be wrong no matter what she did, she studied the shopping directory, found her bearings, and advanced on The Fishmonger's Wife as if she were a very suspicious fishmonger, someone expecting to find a shark, perhaps.

A shark would have been preferable, infinitely so, Anne thought as she cautiously peered round the corner from Mauka Walk to where she could see into the interior of the busy restaurant.

Steele was there, looking cool and comfortable; he'd obviously changed while back at the suite and now wore a pale, expensive-looking lightweight suit that belied his role as a tourist.

And with him, looking equally cool in an extremely chic and stunning outfit that only enhanced her mature loveliness, was Anne's very own wicked stepmother!

Monique? Here? The absurdity of it hammered into Anne's brain. She felt her stomach churn, knew her head was spinning as she stumbled away, nearly crashing through the window of the adjoining jewellery store as she did so.

She made it to the rest-room, though only just. And managed with sternly clenched hands to endure the return bus ride to her hotel before succumbing to another attack of nausea, this one even worse.

That over, she sprawled on the bed with her head spinning and her stomach still contemplating revolt, her only thought to pack and get out, to somehow escape from this nightmare. Her body, however, had other ideas. She was sick again and yet again, running a beaten track between the bathroom and the bed, when the suite door opened and she peered through fevered, delirious, disbelieving eyes to see her father walk into the room.

CHAPTER NINE

'SHE hasn't got the brains God gave a rabbit.'

Steele's voice, booming through the hum of the air-conditioner, resounding off the walls of the hotel suite, a big bass drum in Anne's already throbbing head.

'She has only a touch of sunstroke. A rest, cool, quiet for a bit and she will recover. I do not think a doctor is required.'

Monique's lilting voice, soft, somehow reassuring, if only because it made some sense. Not like Steele.

'She'll have a doctor if I say she'll have a doctor. And I do. Look at the poor girl, damn it!' His voice faded, slightly, as he apparently picked up the telephone and began barking commands into it.

'Men! God gave even the rabbits more brains.' Monique again, as Anne struggled to open her eyes, then struggled in vain to focus on them. Her stomach screamed a warning and she strained to get out of the bed.

'Ah, *chérie*, maybe he is right to call the doctor. Now come, lean on me; we will get there in time,' said that wondrously soft voice, and Anne let her step-mother help her to the bathroom, let her hold her, support her through the inevitable. Let her wipe her face with a damp, wonderfully cold cloth.

A curse in French which needed no translation was shouted into the other room, followed by a scathing indictment on the ancestry of all men in general and

Steele in particular...to be answered by Steele's deep, rich tones.

'I know it's my fault; I left her alone, I never even thought to warn her about wearing a hat.' Deep, rich tones, but tones of anguish; that was unmistakable.

'Of course it is your fault. This entire charade is your fault,' Anne thought she heard, but her step-mother's accent had thickened for some reason, and she found it hard to follow.

Monique helped her back into bed, muttering meanwhile in obviously obscene French/Australian/English. She bathed Anne's fevered brow, muttering all the while, then helped her back through a repeat of the exercise.

After which everything seemed extremely vague. Anne was first sweltering hot, then freezing. Always light-headed, always totally confused. She recognised a stranger's face, heard him speaking in authoritative tones to Monique. She didn't argue with him, took the pills he provided, swallowed the water he gave her, but didn't even try to make sense of it all.

She heard Steele's voice, strangely subdued, thought she heard her father's voice, which made no sense at all and yet did, but she couldn't figure out why.

And then she heard nothing, until she awakened to find her mouth dry and parched, her head still light and throbbing unmercifully, and her limbs so weak she couldn't even lift herself from the bed.

She could, however, manage a croaking plea that brought Monique—yes, it *was* Monique, she realised wonderingly—flying into the room.

'Don't bother to speak; I know,' she said, stooping to help Anne lift herself, guiding her to the bathroom, waiting to ensure she could cope, then helping her back to the bed.

'You must rest,' her stepmother—no longer chic and cultured-looking, but more as Anne remembered her, in shorts and a T-shirt—said with a kindly smile. Biddable as a child, Anne took the tablets, swallowed the water, and drifted off to sleep again under the bliss of that cool towel across her forehead.

Monique was still there when she woke the next time, sitting across the room with a book in her hand, but obviously doing more thinking than reading. Watching through barely opened eyes, Anne secretly observed her stepmother, noting that while Monique was undeniably beautiful, elegant even in only shorts and a T-shirt, there were signs of ageing and hardship that hadn't been there two years earlier.

As if sensing Anne's observation, Monique laid the book aside and rose to come and sit beside her. A hand lifted to touch gently at her forehead, a slow smile gave recognition to the fever's end.

'It is cooler. Good,' Monique said. Then shook her head sadly, the gesture causing ripples in her long, honey-blonde hair, emphasising the compassion in her eyes. 'You really are a silly child,' she said softly. 'Not so stupid as your father and that other grand fool, perhaps, but still very silly. You come out of your winter and go walking all the morning in the sun with no hat; where are your brains? Or has this biggest fool, Steele, stolen them along with your heart?'

Anne allowed her eyes to close, ignoring the question. She couldn't possibly discuss that question with this woman! Monique, as if understanding—and maybe she did, Anne thought—merely added, 'I think maybe so,' before returning to her chair and the assumption that Anne would go back to sleep.

'What... what are you doing here?' Anne finally managed to ask. 'And is my father really here too?'

'Of course he is here. Do you think I would come all this way without him? We are here to see you, to make a grand surprise for you. That, at least, was the wondrous plan created by these two enormously stupid men, anyway.'

'I... I don't understand,' said Anne, who didn't, not at all.

'Nor do I. It is Steele's fault. The great planner has become a... a cropper, I think is the expression. I would say "Hoist with his own petard", but perhaps that is *too* close to the truth. You have, according to him——' and Monique sniffed, making the gesture a most Gallic sneer '—become quite peculiar about this visit to us in Tasmania. He thinks it is because you are nervous about your father being sick, or because you have many guilts. So he telephones and says, "We will meet in Hawaii, which is neutral ground." This, he says, will make it all so much easier for you.'

'But that... that doesn't make any sense. None at all,' Anne replied, trying to rise, failing, trying again.

'Of course it does not,' Monique agreed with another quite Gallic sniff, a gesture Anne had remembered with no fondness, but which now seemed somehow comforting. 'I tried to tell him that *he* was the problem, but he is like your father—they don't listen to me until it is too late. And stop trying to get up; it is not necessary, and, according to the doctor, not advised.'

'The doctor... oh, yes, I remember. He made me take pills and gave you all sorts of instructions.'

'One of which was to think about throwing you into a very cold bath for a very long time, but fortunately that was not necessary. Although it might have been good for you. What were you thinking about, walking in this sun with no protection?'

'I was...thinking,' Anne hedged. 'And of course it was stupid; I know that. I just...didn't think.' She essayed a giggle at how ridiculous that must all sound, but stopped immediately because her headache didn't approve.

'Steele's fault. He was supposed to be taking care of you, and he goes off walking too, by himself. At least he had the sense to do it at night, without the sun. *Only* that much sense, mind you.'

All of which made even less sense to Anne, and was less relevant than what she really wanted to know.

'But what about my father?' she demanded. 'He was supposed to be...'

'Sick? He was. Perhaps will be again, although perhaps not. We can only hope.'

'Dying,' Anne said, concerned by her stepmother's seemingly unconcerned attitude.

'We are all doing that,' was the curious reply. 'Only some of us are so stupid we read too many magazine articles about it and then try to be our own doctors and...well...I will let him tell you. I will *make* him tell you,' Monique added with a sudden savageness. 'It can be part of his punishment for being such a stupid man. But not now. Now I will get you something cold to drink and you can go back to sleep.'

'But I'm fine now,' Anne protested. 'If all I got is a bit too much sun...'

'And not enough to drink, so that you are dehydrated. When too much sun is so bad that you need a doctor, then you must do what the doctor says, and he says you will stay in bed until tomorrow,' Monique continued implacably, throwing the words over her shoulder as she went to refill the jug of water from beside the bed, then returned to insist that Anne drink. 'You cannot see your father in any event until to-morrow because—I hope—he and that fool Steele are asleep. Or else they are out drinking, in which case this whole expedition has been a waste. Steele probably *is* out drinking; he has been so worried about you he is not capable of much else.'

And then, with a surprisingly gentle, sad smile, she said, 'Maybe it is *we* who are the stupid ones, *chérie*. We bring our men to this romantic tropical paradise and then force them to sleep with each other. It is even crazier than walking in the sun, eh? You sleep now; in the morning all will be better.'

She was leaving the room even as Anne protested, but hardly had the door shut before Anne's eyes followed suit. The next thing she knew it was morning, a glorious, sunshine morning that she felt capable of dealing with.

She stole out of the bed and into the bathroom, where she luxuriated in a long, cool, wonderful shower before padding over to sit on the balcony, wrapped in a huge bath-towel as she drank half the jug of tropical fruit juice she found in the refrigerator. Thirst temporarily assuaged, she changed into a halter-top and shorts, and was back on the balcony brushing her hair when there was a gentle tap at the door.

She opened it to find her father, looking every inch the tourist, in a blistering Hawaiian print shirt and a pair of very baggy shorts.

'Breakfast will be up in a few minutes,' he said, seemingly almost afraid to face her. But then he reached out to gather her in his arms and hug her as if he might never have another chance.

'God, but it's good to see you,' he finally said, and to Anne's surprise he was fighting back tears. 'I've caused you a lot of grief, I'm told, and I'm really, really sorry, Anne.'

'You caused me some worry, but it wasn't you that caused the grief,' she replied. 'Although you would have, if you'd died. And——' stepping back and eyeing him up and down '—you don't look much like a dying man to me. What's going on, anyway?'

He snorted, and the gesture was so like Monique's that Anne nearly laughed. 'You mean that silly woman hasn't told you? I'm surprised; she's told everybody else. Thinks it's hilarious, she does. Great French cow!'

'I will pretend not to have heard that,' said Monique's voice from behind them as she emerged from the suite's other bedroom. Steele's bedroom, Anne thought, with a curious little lurch to her tummy. 'But only if you have ordered breakfast for me too. With croissants.'

'Would I ever fail you?' Curtis asked, his eyes gleaming with an adoration so obvious that it made Anne uncomfortable, knowing what she knew.

'Frequently,' was the response, but surely those hooded green eyes held a similar gleam of affection? Anne thought. And became further confused when Monique languidly strolled over to deposit a loving kiss upon her husband's cheek before moving with equal grace to the bathroom and blowing them both a kiss before she shut the door behind her.

The door was flung open again almost immediately, however, so that Monique could shake a fierce forefinger and demand, 'And see that you tell her *everything*—the whole stupidity! I shall be listening, and if you don't you can sleep with Steele again tonight.'

'Everything' took quite a while. Monique joined them for breakfast before her husband got through his sheepish tale of having prostate problems that he thought was cancer, of refusing to see the doctor because he was too frightened—and too confused, added Monique, who had joined them by this time—of finding his writing going badly and only starting to come good when he'd listened to what he described as 'Monique's total and utter uninterest' when they'd spoken to Anne by telephone.

'Of course, once I saw the quack, it turned out the prostate thing was pretty minor after all. I didn't even need to get hacked apart or anything; just medicine.'

'So... I didn't really need to come after all,' Anne said, suspicion rampant in her mind. 'Steele knew all this before we even left Canada. He would have. He *must* have, if he's been able to phone and arrange for you to be here!'

'Steele,' Monique sniffed, 'does not know what day it is. He plots and schemes, and he is a romantic fool. And when his plans come unstuck, which they have done in Canada, and I am sure it was *his* fault, he is on the telephone to me for help. Me! It is not enough I have this old man to deal with, I have Steele blathering on about children. What did you do to him, *chérie*—get angry and tell him you were barren, like me?'

Anne's ears took in the words; her mind processed them. But after that it all disappeared in a kaleidoscope of insanity. What Monique had said made no sense. None of it, but most especially the last part.

'B-b-barren?' she cried. 'But I heard...he said...it just can't be!'

'Ah.' Monique looked at Anne, her eyes soft now, compelling. 'I have come closer to the mark than I wished, perhaps? You *are* barren, but you have not told him, *could* not tell him. It is hardly the end of the world, *chérie*. Not for a man like that.'

'No...no, it isn't that,' Anne replied, then faltered and couldn't go on. Not with her father sitting there listening avidly. He'll probably put this in a book, she found herself thinking quite irrelevantly.

Monique was quick on the uptake. 'Out,' she demanded with an imperious gesture at her startled husband. 'Go and find that fool Steele and take him shopping. He likes that. Tell him if I see him before he has bought many presents, expensive presents, presents for *both* of us, I will cut off his...you know! And feed them to him in the wallaby stew. I may do it anyway. Now go...go on.' And he fled as she flapped her arms in the air and continued to threaten him with quite awful things.

'Now,' Monique said when Curtis had safely left the room. 'Now you will tell me everything, every little detail. And I warn you, *chérie*, that I think I am going to laugh and laugh and laugh.'

It took a bit of hedging and backing and filling, and not a little outright threatening by Monique, but Anne finally managed to detail what she'd heard and how she had reacted.

Monique howled, laughing so thoroughly that she fell off her chair and frightened Anne half to death. Then she looked at Anne again, fought to maintain her composure, and burst out laughing worse than before.

'And you thought... oh, this is too funny. Your father must hear this. Steele must hear this. You thought... oh... oh... oh! Never again will either of them dare to criticise *my* English. Never!'

'But... but he *said* that,' Anne protested. 'He said exactly that.'

'But of course he did. Oh, Anne, you are silly as your father, whom I love very much and you will *not* tell him I said so. Steele said that, of course, but you listened only to the *words*! I have been telling him it for years, since you were there with us at home and he fell in love with you.'

Anne faltered. Steele... in love with *her*? 'But... but he said you...'

'He said *we*, and since he was with you when he said it, you stupid girl, he meant *you*—you and he... him. He said that I have been telling him you and he should have half a dozen children, because you both love them so much. Hah! Love is not only blind, it is stupid too.'

'But what did he mean about circumstances maybe changing?' Anne asked, getting cranky now because she felt so incredibly stupid, so totally ridiculous. And so ashamed.

That Gallic shrug. 'Probably that he was planning and scheming because your father's stupidity has given Steele the excuse he needed to bring you back to Tasmania, to ensure that you will like it, so when you are married you will want to stay there with him.'

'But ... but why would he think that I wouldn't?'

'Because you and your stupid, stubborn father had so much trouble getting along when you were here that you did not have a chance to even think about that? Because Steele thought, being a bigger fool even than your father, that you were too young, that you needed to go back to Canada to be able to make a comparison? How should I know, and does it matter anyway?

Monique rose, strode around the table, and took Anne in her arms. 'If I could have a daughter, I would be proud if she was you,' she said, then stepped back and glared fiercely at her, shaking her finger in her face.

'But I tell you now that I am finished with this matchmaking. Finished! I am too old for this and it makes me too ... cranky. Men are such fools, and romantic men are even worse. If you want Steele—you take him. And you keep him! But you do not come running to me every time the romantic fool does something which upsets you. Agreed?'

'Agreed,' Anne replied, hardly able to see her no-longer-wicked stepmother through the tears that poured down her face.

'*Bon*. We will have coffee now, and when these men of ours return we shall admire their presents and then we shall take them out to buy *more* presents. Agreed?'

'*Not* agreed!' Anne declared firmly. 'You and Dad can go and do whatever you like, but Steele can get *his* presents right here.'

'Good,' said her stepmother. 'Now you are learning. I have decided I do not want coffee after all. I am going now. *My* present will be your father's laughter when I tell him this.'

She kissed Anne quickly on both cheeks, then strode to the door and away, blowing Anne a flamboyant kiss as she departed.

Anne did have coffee. She was ready for it; she needed the pause to think about everything, to try and still the bubbling excitement that banished all vestiges of her sunstroke. She drank the coffee, spent considerable time in the bathroom removing the ravages of her earlier tears, then spent even more experimenting with the sarong to ensure the best possible wrapping for Steele's present—the wrapping which undid the easiest.

Steele took one look, when he arrived a few minutes later with her father in tow, both men with their arms laden with gaily wrapped gifts, then turned and eased the older man out of the door faster than he'd come in.

'That,' he said with eyes that shone their pleasure, 'must be the finest present I've ever bought.'

'This,' Anne replied, doing a quick twirl that failed to hide how close to tears she was, but showed off the sarong to its best advantage, 'is only the wrapping.'

'Does that mean I don't need all these?' he asked, nodding at the mound of parcels that filled both arms. He moved towards her, then turned aside, prepared to deposit the packages on the sofa.

'Certainly not,' she said. 'Although I really don't deserve any of them. Will you ever forgive me for being such a fool?'

'I'll forgive you anything, but you'll have to let me put these damned parcels down first,' he said.

'Well,' she sighed, 'I suppose you'll have to if you're going to unwrap your present. But before you do,' she added as the parcels landed in a heap on the sofa and Steele strode not quite near enough to touch her, 'there's another present on your pillow you might want to look at first.'

He raised one eyebrow, then nodded his acceptance and walked briskly into his bedroom, whence a howl of laughter erupted, followed by total silence. And he didn't come back.

When curiosity got the better of Anne, she opened the door to find him sprawled on the bed, wearing *only* his other present and a broad grin.

'Shopping is such damned hard work,' he explained. 'I thought maybe I should be lying down before I attempted to unwrap any more parcels.'

'That,' said Anne, 'sounds like a very good idea to me. I'll just bring all those others in, shall I?'

'They can wait; I can't,' he growled, out of the bed and holding her in his arms before she had a chance to move. His lips descended to claim her mouth, his hands lifted her to fit her body against his. When he finally spoke again, his breathing was as ragged as her own.

'Although,' he whispered, 'the best part of presents is the unwrapping.'

'Not this time,' Anne whispered in reply. 'This time, the best is yet to come.'

And it was.

HARLEQUIN ROMANCE®

brings you

More Romances Celebrating Love, Families and Children!

We promised in December, after bringing you
The Nutcracker Prince and **The Santa Sleuth**,
that we would have more wonderful titles in our
KIDS & KISSES series. True to our promise, in January
we have the wonderfully warm story **No Ties**
(Harlequin Romance #3344) by Rosemary Gibson. When
Cassie goes to work for Professor Adam Merrick, she finds
not only love and marriage, but a ready-made family!

Watch for more of these special romances from favorite
Harlequin Romance authors in the coming months:

February	#3347	A Valentine for Daisy	Betty Neels
March	#3351	Leonie's Luck	Emma Goldrick
April	#3357	The Baby Business	Rebecca Winters
May	#3359	Bachelor's Family	Jessica Steele

Available wherever Harlequin books are sold.

KIDS8

This January, Harlequin and Silhouette
proudly bring you

by Request™

Stranded!

When you're stranded, should you trust your head or
your heart?

Three complete novels by your favorite authors—in
one special collection!

THE SILVER SNARE by Stephanie James
FLASHPOINT by Patricia Gardner Evans
A STRANGER'S SMILE by Kathleen Korbel

Trapped alone with a stranger...the perfect place for
suspicion, tension *and* romance!

Available wherever
Harlequin and Silhouette books are sold.

HARLEQUIN®   **Silhouette®**

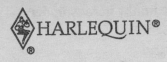HARLEQUIN®

The proprietors of Weddings, Inc. hope you have enjoyed visiting Eternity, Massachusetts. And if you missed any of the exciting Weddings, Inc. titles, here is your opportunity to complete your collection:

Harlequin Superromance	#598	*Wedding Invitation* by Marisa Carroll	$3.50 U.S. ☐ $3.99 CAN. ☐
Harlequin Romance	#3319	*Expectations* by Shannon Waverly	$2.99 U.S. ☐ $3.50 CAN. ☐
Harlequin Temptation	#502	*Wedding Song* by Vicki Lewis Thompson	$2.99 U.S. ☐ $3.50 CAN. ☐
Harlequin American Romance	#549	*The Wedding Gamble* by Muriel Jensen	$3.50 U.S. ☐ $3.99 CAN. ☐
Harlequin Presents	#1692	*The Vengeful Groom* by Sara Wood	$2.99 U.S. ☐ $3.50 CAN. ☐
Harlequin Intrigue	#298	*Edge of Eternity* by Jasmine Cresswell	$2.99 U.S. ☐ $3.50 CAN. ☐
Harlequin Historical	#248	*Vows* by Margaret Moore	$3.99 U.S. ☐ $4.50 CAN. ☐

HARLEQUIN BOOKS...
NOT THE SAME OLD STORY

TOTAL AMOUNT	$
POSTAGE & HANDLING ($1.00 for one book, 50¢ for each additional)	$
APPLICABLE TAXES*	$ _____
TOTAL PAYABLE (check or money order—please do not send cash)	$ _____

To order, complete this form and send it, along with a check or money order for the total above, payable to Harlequin Books, to: **In the U.S.:** 3010 Walden Avenue, P.O. Box 9047, Buffalo, NY 14269-9047; **In Canada:** P.O. Box 613, Fort Erie, Ontario, L2A 5X3.

Name: _____

Address: _____ City: _____

State/Prov.: _____ Zip/Postal Code: _____

*New York residents remit applicable sales taxes.
 Canadian residents remit applicable GST and provincial taxes.

WED-F

This holiday, join four hunky heroes under the mistletoe for

Christmas Kisses

Cuddle under a fluffy quilt, with a cup of hot chocolate and these romances sure to warm you up:

#561 HE'S A REBEL (also a Studs title)
Linda Randall Wisdom

#562 THE BABY AND THE BODYGUARD
Jule McBride

#563 THE GIFT-WRAPPED GROOM
M.J. Rodgers

#564 A TIMELESS CHRISTMAS
Pat Chandler

Celebrate the season with all four holiday books sealed with a Christmas kiss—coming to you in December, only from Harlequin American Romance!

CHRISTMAS STALKINGS

All wrapped up in spine-tingling packages, here are three books guaranteed to chill your spine...and warm your hearts this holiday season!

#302 THE KID WHO STOLE CHRISTMAS
Linda Stevens

#303 I'LL BE HOME FOR CHRISTMAS
Dawn Stewardson

#304 BEARING GIFTS
Aimée Thurlo

This December, fill your stockings with the "Christmas Stalkings"—for the best in romantic suspense. Only from

HARLEQUIN®

INTRIGUE®

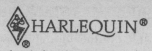

HARLEQUIN®

Don't miss these Harlequin favorites by some of our most distinguished authors!
And now you can receive a discount by ordering two or more titles!

HT#25483	BABYCAKES by Glenda Sanders	$2.99	☐
HT#25559	JUST ANOTHER PRETTY FACE by Candace Schuler	$2.99	☐
HP#11608	SUMMER STORMS by Emma Goldrick	$2.99	☐
HP#11632	THE SHINING OF LOVE by Emma Darcy	$2.99	☐
HR#03265	HERO ON THE LOOSE by Rebecca Winters	$2.89	☐
HR#03268	THE BAD PENNY by Susan Fox	$2.99	☐
HS#70532	TOUCH THE DAWN by Karen Young	$3.39	☐
HS#70576	ANGELS IN THE LIGHT by Margot Dalton	$3.50	☐
HI#22249	MUSIC OF THE MIST by Laura Pender	$2.99	☐
HI#22267	CUTTING EDGE by Caroline Burnes	$2.99	☐
HAR#16489	DADDY'S LITTLE DIVIDEND by Elda Minger	$3.50	☐
HAR#16525	CINDERMAN by Anne Stuart	$3.50	☐
HH#28801	PROVIDENCE by Miranda Jarrett	$3.99	☐
HH#28775	A WARRIOR'S QUEST by Margaret Moore (limited quantities available on certain titles)	$3.99	☐

TOTAL AMOUNT	$
DEDUCT: 10% DISCOUNT FOR 2+ BOOKS	$
POSTAGE & HANDLING ($1.00 for one book, 50¢ for each additional)	$
APPLICABLE TAXES*	$_____
TOTAL PAYABLE	$_____
(check or money order—please do not send cash)	

To order, complete this form and send it, along with a check or money order for the total above, payable to Harlequin Books, to: **In the U.S.:** 3010 Walden Avenue, P.O. Box 9047, Buffalo, NY 14269-9047; **In Canada:** P.O. Box 613, Fort Erie, Ontario, L2A 5X3.

Name: _____

Address: _____ City: _____

State/Prov.: _____ Zip/Postal Code: _____

*New York residents remit applicable sales taxes.
 Canadian residents remit applicable GST and provincial taxes.